PRISM

Joan Bochmann
and
Janet Muirhead Hill

Raven Publishing, Inc.
Norris, MT

PRISM

Raven Publishing, Inc. PO Box 2866, Norris, MT 59745

www.ravenpublishing.net

ISBN: 978-1-937849-65-8

Printed in the United States

Library of Congress Cataloging-in-Publication Data

Names: Bochmann, Joan, author. | Hill, Janet Muirhead, author.
Title: Prism / Joan M. Bochmann and Janet M. Hill.
Description: Norris, MT : Raven Publishing, Inc., [2020] |
Summary: "Debra Randall, daughter of aircraft mogul, Josh Randall is missing, and Lieutenant Garrigan of the San Francisco police department is baffled. At first, he'd assumed it was a kidnapping. Now he's not sure. The three men in her life: her father; her best friend from childhood, Paul Diamond; and her estranged boyfriend, Blake Mallory, each seem to be holding something back."-- Provided by publisher."
Identifiers: LCCN 2020009549 (print) | LCCN 2020009550 (ebook) | ISBN 9781937849658 (paperback) | ISBN 9781937849665 (ebook)
Subjects: GSAFD: Mystery fiction.
Classification: LCC PS3602.O3253 P75 2020 (print) | LCC PS3602. O3253 (ebook) | DDC 813/.6--dc23
LC record available at https://lccn.loc.gov/2020009549
LC ebook record available at https://lccn.loc.gov/2020009550

Critical Acclaim for PRISM

"PRISM is a gripping story of searching and longing—both the physical search for Debra Randall, the missing daughter of the richest man in California, and the emotional search for the key to unlock the Randall family secrets. These two storylines braid together throughout the book as Debra's boyfriend, Blake, her best friend, Paul, and her distant father, Josh, set out to find out what happened to her, embarking on a twisting, turning search for clues from Canada to Mexico. Does her disappearance involve her work helping draft dodgers escape the Vietnam War? Is it related to her trance-like "spells" or the violent drug dealer she gets mixed up with? Or might one of the three men in her life be responsible for her disappearance? The puzzle pieces include hermits and New Age cults, love triangles and torture chambers, with plenty of danger lurking at every hairpin turn. A good mystery keeps us guessing, and PRISM keeps us guessing until we reach the satisfying end."
— **Elise Atchison**, author of *Crazy Mountain*, winner of the Eludia Award and the Barbara Deming Memorial Fund Award.

"Prism is a vibrant and mysterious story of loss and fear. The reader will be drawn in, layer by layer, as a young woman's friends race against time to discover what led to her disappearance. Their quest is stymied at every turn, leading the searchers to uncover as many questions as answers. Janet Hill has done a magnificent job of completing Joan Bochmann's work, and there's no doubt her sister would be proud." — **Lorretta Lynde**, Author, *Magpie Odyssey Series*

"This fine novel is interesting on several levels: as a riveting crime case, a view of the troubled Vietnam War era, and the policies and effects of the military draft as viewed from two generations. It's an intricate missing person case, an example of how mental health crises can impact families and friends, and a touching love story.

"This book is a collaboration between two sister-authors. Janet Muirhead Hill's readable and involving writing combines with the plot, characters, and unfinished manuscript of her beloved late sister, Joan Bochmann. This good book, PRISM, honors both of the sister-writers." — **Marcia Melton**, author of *The Boarding House, Joe Henry's Journey, Joe Henry's Return*, and *Nighthawk's Harmonica*.

"Debra Randall is gone. Her father, her boyfriend, and her best friend—all men who love her, each in his own way—are devastated. From California to Texas to Colorado to Canada, the search goes on. Detective Patrick Garrigan investigates every facet, certain that each of the men in Ms. Randall's life is withholding something, and for each of them it is personal and unique, each secret holding an important key…including the necklace she wears, a chunk of glass shaped like a pyramid that seems to send her into a trance or hypnotic state. So many questions that take him and the men in her life on a journey they weren't expecting." — **James Paddock**, author of *Saving Ebony* and *Webbed Secrets*

"When Debra Randall goes missing, the three men closest to her give less than satisfying answers to the San Francisco detective's questions. Her father, a wealthy airplane manufacturer, shows impatience. Her life-long friend Paul, a co-worker at the city's newspaper, doesn't mention that the prism Debra often wears isn't among the jewelry left behind in her apartment. Blake, who calls himself 'just a friend,' tries to hide emotions that suggest he's much closer than that. He and Debra are pilots.

"The story opens in February 1972, with characters' back stories carefully woven in. Author Janet Muirhead Hill, best known for her children's and young-adult books, honored her sister, Joan Bochmann's request to complete this story after Joan's death." — **Jan Walker**, author of both fiction and prison education works

Memories, murder, and mystery woven into a tangled web of stories within a story. Unusual and intriguing. — **Heidi M. Thomas**, award-winning author of the *Cowgirl Dreams* series, *American Dream* series, and *Cowgirl Up: A History of Rodeo Women*.

This intriguing missing-persons story contains many elements beyond the mystery. PRISM has an intricate plot, and presents complex family dynamics with its well-defined characters. Strong writing! — **Kae Cheatham**, Editor and Author of *Hammer Come Down* and other published titles.

Dedicated to Joan's children,
Gary Zimmerman and Debra Tanner,
In fond memory of
Joan Bochmann
loving mother, grandmother, sister, friend, and mentor
who is sorely missed by all who knew her.

PROLOGUE

She slips silently through the grove of aspen trees and kneels by the clear mountain stream. Motionless, she studies her rippling reflection in the water. Slender and green-eyed with straight blond hair falling below her shoulders, she's dressed in blue jeans and a plaid shirt. The shirt's open at the neck, revealing a fine gold chain from which a small pyramid-shaped crystal is suspended. As she watches her reflection, her slim fingers stray to the prism, and she begins exploring all its facets. She holds it up and watches its colors bloom and spin.

When her gaze returns to her reflection, she gasps. The prism slips from her fingers. The image looking back at her is changing. The hair is darker, curlier, and lies softly around a face that is hers, yet not quite. Her shirt and jeans morph into a gown of a floating, wispy material.

"No," she moans, knowing she must turn away but cannot. "Go away," she whispers. "Please."

CHAPTER 1

Patrick Garrigan stood at the doorway of the police station for a moment before stepping into the cold San Francisco drizzle. It was February 17, 1972, and he was tired. As he unlocked his car, he noticed a tremor in his hand. *I'm getting too old for this kind of work.* He thought longingly of the vacation he planned—Oregon wilderness, salmon fishing, and best of all, no people. He started the car.

Sliding into traffic, he sighed. *I'll be lucky if I get this case wrapped up by then,* he thought, even though his vacation was scheduled for June, four months away. It had seemed so routine a week ago—just another missing person. People in this town disappeared all the time. Sometimes you found their bodies, sometimes you did not. What made this one so bizarre was—damn it, he wasn't sure what it was. He did know it was getting to him. At first, he had been sure it was a kidnapping. Not only did Debra Randall have a very rich daddy, she had made quite a name for herself in her own right. She had written some really good stuff during her career with the *Examiner*. He had reread a lot of it last night, and some of her features were rather moving. It had been two weeks since she'd gone missing, and there had been nothing—no note, no phone call, no demands whatsoever. Normally, that would rule out kidnapping. However, if the kidnappers' purpose was to kill her, that would be something else altogether.

He'd pored over files, looking for anyone who might

have a grudge against her—a mighty big grudge, but had come up empty. Unless... He remembered something about her college days. As a feature reporter, she had been involved in some kind of anti-war activity, but he couldn't remember just what it was. There was a lot of tension between protesters and vets. Maybe a veteran, his mind twisted by Vietnam, had lost control and taken revenge.

It didn't fit. There was nothing anywhere, no evidence at all, to indicate any sort of foul play. Her apartment looked as if she had just run out to get the paper. That also ruled out voluntary disappearance. It didn't look like anything was missing. Clothes, jewelry, everything seemed intact. *Well,* Garrigan thought, *maybe we'll find out tonight.*

Parking in front of the luxurious apartment building, Garrigan started up the walk. His job didn't bring him to this neighborhood often. The snooty uniformed door-man looked at him with barely disguised distaste as he held the door for him. Garrigan stepped in, noticing that the three men he was meeting were already waiting in the lobby. He paused to study the unlikely trio before they noticed him.

Josh Randall, whom he recognized from photographs, was 60 but could have passed for 45 or 50. He had the suave good looks that often grace the very rich—dark hair with just enough gray at the temples to be distinguishing. Cool and aloof, he looked at his watch. The only sign of stress Garrigan observed was the agony in Randall's jade-green eyes.

Paul Diamond was different. He came off as a man possessed, restlessly pacing the lobby. It was Paul, a newspaper coworker, who had reported Debra missing. Garrigan had since learned that they grew up together. He was the tallest of the three. Despite his expensive clothes, he looked disheveled. The ravages of the last two weeks showed plainly on his face.

The third man, dressed in Levis and a sheepskin-lined, leather coat, leaned against the wall near the elevator. His tan made the other men look pale. Blake Mallory was "just a friend," he'd said. Garrigan wondered. He'd been instantly suspicious of this one, but that suspicion was lessening. For all his brooding composure, something in his eyes convinced Garrigan that Mallory was suffering as much or more than the other two.

Garrigan stepped out of the shadows and approached the men. Diamond stopped pacing and looked at him, hope naked on his face.

"About time, Garrigan." Josh Randall punched the elevator button impatiently, and the door slid open.

Garrigan shrugged.

"Any word, Lieutenant?" Paul asked, as they entered.

Garrigan shook his head, watching the elevator panel blink off the floors. The elevator stopped, and the door slid open, revealing a short, carpeted hallway, leading directly to ornate double doors. Pausing at the doors, the detective turned to the three men.

"As I understand it, each of you has been here before, right?"

"Of course," Josh snapped.

"A couple of times," Paul said.

Mallory merely nodded.

Unlocking the door, the detective motioned the men inside. The apartment contrasted sharply with the somber colors of the hallway. Everything was light and airy. An array of plants and broad windows gave the illusion of being outside.

Garrigan took off his topcoat and turned toward the three men who were surveying the room as if waiting for its owner to appear and invite them to sit down.

"Mr. Randall?" Garrigan thought the man flinched, but he couldn't be sure. "Tell me, please; when was the last time you were in this room."

Josh frowned. "Over a year ago, I guess. At Christmas. That'd be 1970."

Garrigan made a note in his ever-present spiral notepad.

"Mr. Diamond?"

Paul hesitated only a moment. "Two weeks ago. Friday. The day before Deb disappeared."

Garrigan raised one bushy red eyebrow. "How do you know she disappeared on Saturday? Did she normally work Saturdays?"

"Not normally, but often. I called her Saturday and there was no answer. You see, she'd just returned from a short vacation and was working on a feature for the Sunday edition. She had promised to have it in by noon. Debra never missed a deadline. Never."

Garrigan nodded and then made another notation.

"When did you contact us, Mr. Diamond?" Garrigan knew very well that the Department didn't receive a report until late Monday afternoon.

"Well, not until Monday. I thought maybe something had come up. But when I couldn't reach her all weekend and she didn't show up at work Monday..." Paul's voice broke.

4

Garrigan nodded again and turned to Mallory, who was staring at a photograph on the television set—a picture of Debra, her hair blowing in the breeze, standing beside the Randall Rustler, a twin-engine airplane her father had designed. It was a black and white glossy—probably taken by a newspaper photographer. He made a note to ask Paul about it.

"Mr. Mallory?"

Blake tore his eyes from the picture, and Garrigan caught the tortured look he had glimpsed earlier. Mallory quickly composed his features into a mask and said, "Last Thursday."

"What?" Garrigan was aware that both Paul and Randall had echoed his question.

"I was here last Thursday," Mallory said calmly. "Right after I was finally informed that Debra was missing." Mallory looked at Josh Randall with barely controlled fury.

The detective said, "You mean..."

"Don't worry, Garrigan," Blake interrupted. "Your men did their job. They didn't let me past her front door."

Garrigan made another notation. Why in hell hadn't that encounter been in the report?

"Okay, before that, when was the last time you were in this apartment?"

"About a month ago. I think it was around the second."

Garrigan made more notes, sat down in a large cream-colored chair, and motioned the men to be seated. Paul sat on the couch facing the detective, and Mallory sank into the wing to Garrigan's chair. Josh Randall remained standing.

5

"Sit down, Mr. Randall, please."

"Look, Garrigan, what is this all about? What are we supposed to be doing here?"

"My men have combed this apartment. There is no sign of forced entry, no sign of a struggle. The only fingerprints belong to Debra Randall or the three of you, with the exception of a couple which have been identified as your wife's."

"We know all that, Garrigan."

Detective Garrigan was becoming well aware that Josh Randall didn't like him much.

"As far as we can tell, nothing has been taken. We found, as you know, a considerable amount of money, jewelry, art objects, silver, what have you. Nothing appears to have been disturbed," Garrigan explained. "However, we can't really know what all Miss Randall had here. That's why I asked all of you to come. I want you to look through this apartment and tell me if there's anything—anything at all—that is missing."

CHAPTER 2

Blake Mallory sat at the little desk in the corner of Debra's bright yellow kitchen. He hated what they were doing. Rummaging through her things—raping her privacy. He rubbed the antique, cherry-wood desk absently and tried not to think of Paul Diamond in Debra's bedroom. Had he been there before? He had desperately wanted to ask her that. He had never understood Debra's relationship with Paul, despite her patient explanations.

"For Heaven's sake, Blake," she'd said. "We grew up together. I tagged after him everywhere most of my life. He was the one constant I had. When Daddy would fly off after the weekend, Paul was always there to comfort me."

"Just like a big brother, huh?"

"Yes. Just like a brother." But she'd looked away when she said it.

"He doesn't look at you as if you were a sister, Debra. And you know it."

"Oh, shush!"

And that was as far as they ever got. He knew his probing jealousy was hurting their relationship, but he couldn't seem to help it.

He opened the center drawer of the desk. Its contents were a jumble of paper clips, rubber bands, an earring, pens, pencils, and little scraps of paper with scribbled notes and phone numbers.

"Looking for anything in particular, Mallory?" Garrigan asked.

"Yeah. Her logbook. Debra's a pilot. If she planned to be gone anytime at all, she would have taken her logbook."

"Good thinking," Garrigan complimented. "You're a pilot yourself, aren't you?"

"Yeah."

Yeah, I'm a pilot, Blake thought. *I may not have the foggiest idea what else I am, but that much I know.* He wondered if that was what had first attracted him to the slim, beautiful girl whose possessions they were now violating. He remembered the night he met her.

He had been working late at the little fixed-base operation he and the bank owned, when Josh Randall's plane had taxied to a stop in front of the ramshackle hangar.

"Hey, you," Randall yelled. "Service this plane and put it in a hangar. You got a car?"

"Who the hell are you, the Shah of Iran?" Blake asked.

Josh whirled and stared at him, disbelievingly.

"What's your name, boy?"

"I'm not a boy."

"What's your name, damn it?"

"Blake Mallory. What's yours?"

"Josh Randall. Now, if you want to have a job fifteen minutes from now, I suggest you get the lead out and do as I say."

Blake hated that tone. He'd heard it all his life.

"You go straight to hell, Mr. Josh Randall." He turned back to the Cessna he was working on. He felt Randall's hand on his shoulder and tightened his grip on his wrench. Randall dropped his hand but didn't back away.

"Where's your boss?" Randall rasped.

"You're lookin' at him."

"You own this operation? But, you're just a kid."

Blake didn't answer, and they stared at each other for several seconds, wills clashing.

"Look, Mallory. I'd love to stay and teach you some manners, but I'm late for my daughter's graduation. Now would you be kind enough to service my plane and loan me a car?"

Blake noticed the aircraft for the first time and felt a thrill of admiration.

"That's a beauty! What is it?"

"A Randall Rustler. Now, how about that car?"

"You built it?"

Randall nodded.

Blake threw Josh the keys.

"The Chevy pickup over there. Have it back here at 10:00."

He remembered watching the lights approach the building. He'd expected Randall to be deliberately late, but it was only 9:45. He stood in the darkened doorway of his office as the pickup rolled to a stop. He heard her laugh before he saw her. It was a lovely sound, clear and bubbly. Moving for a better view, he came face to face with a beautiful young lady. Tall, slender, with a cloud of blond hair and clear, emerald eyes, she smiled at him.

"Hi." She extended her hand.

"Hi." He took it and noticed she smelled as wonderful as she looked.

Josh came around to the front of the truck.

"Mallory, my daughter, Debra."

Blake released her hand reluctantly and looked at

Josh. "Your plane is ready. I didn't have any hangar space, so it's tied down over there."

Josh frowned. "Lucky for you it didn't hail."

Blake looked at the starlit sky and grinned. "Yeah, lucky for me."

Debra laughed. "Mallory. Is that your whole name?"

"Blake."

"Where are you from, Blake? If you'd been here long, I'd have found you by now."

Nothing in Blake's experience had quite prepared him for this forthright, friendly girl.

"Colorado."

"Well, why don't you come with us? I have a graduation party waiting at the ranch."

"No. Thanks, anyway, but I couldn't."

"Why not?"

Blake looked from his grease-smudged jeans to Debra's white dress and shook his head.

"C'mon. There's a good band, lots of girls. Give you a chance to meet some people."

"I don't think so. Thanks, anyway."

Debra was thoughtful for a moment. "You can ride left seat and fly the Rustler."

How had she known that was the most persuasive thing she could have said?

He opened another drawer and removed a thick manuscript. This must be the book she had been working on— the one she was so secretive about.

"Of course I want you to read it, Blake. You will be the first. It's just that I can't show it to you until its finished—it isn't good enough yet."

Blake's heart raced as he scanned the first page.

THE CANADIAN ODYSSEY
by
D. Randall

The early morning mission began like all the
others at the meeting in Ellen's kitchen with
young men desperate to escape the lottery
ticket they'd just won. Prize: the chance to
sacrifice their lives in a war they did not
believe in, taking place in a jungle they never
wanted to see.

He riffled through the remaining pages to see if it was
what he thought it was.

Oh, Debra. You naïve child. His fingers shook. How
could she? *You said you were writing a novel, but this
looks like an exact account of what we fell into in Canada, our well-kept secret—kept for your safety. Oh, my
darling, don't you see how dangerous it is to put it on
paper?*

Blake knew that when she began almost two years ago,
Debra viewed that dangerous, secret mission as a time of
her greatest heroism, just as she had looked upon their
cargo as fervent idealists. Had anyone else known what
she was writing about? Could they have guessed? Blake
felt sick with fear as he thought about his brother.

"Find her logbook, Mallory?" Garrigan called from
the living room.

Blake stuffed the manuscript back into the desk as the
detective entered the room.

"Not yet." He pulled open another drawer.

There it was. A small well-worn black book with Deb-

11

ra's name embossed in the corner. The gold embossing was rubbing off: DEB A RAN AL. Blake flipped to the page with the latest entry. January 14 SFRO – LA – SFRO. He handed the book to Garrigan.

CHAPTER 3

Josh Randall moved through the rooms of his daughter's lavish apartment, fighting the rage that always seemed to grip him when he was not in control. What had happened to her, anyway? Was it his fault somehow? Probably. He hadn't been a good father; he knew that. Oh, he had provided for her all right—very well in fact. She always had anything she wanted from paper dolls to flying lessons. Yet when his memories of Debra as a child surfaced, they were always of a tear-stained face, begging him not to go off and leave her. How do you explain to a motherless child that you have to make a living? More than that—that designing and building airplanes is your very oxygen—your link with life. She had been a good child, considering that she was raised by a series of housekeepers. The only times he remembered being angry with her was when she pestered him to tell her about her mother. And that anger had been irrational; he knew that. She had no way of knowing the pain her questions evoked.

Where was she now? Was she hurt? Somehow, he just couldn't believe something had happened to her. She must have just gone off somewhere.

He had been sure she had gone back to Texas, but a call to his foreman had ruled that out. No one had seen her.

Josh looked at the bookcases lining the living room wall. She certainly loved books. He was unfamiliar with many of the titles. He never had time to read. Only the aeronautical engineering textbooks he had given her and the classics he had only heard about struck a responsive chord. At the end of the top row was a cluster of framed snapshots. Several of him in various poses, taken the year he gave Debra her first camera, and one of Paul on the buckskin mare Josh had given him when he was ten. He frowned at one of Blake and Debra, arms entwined, mugging at the camera.

At the sight of the next picture, his heart leapt—where in the hell? He looked closer. It was Diana! He had never kept any pictures of his wife. There'd been damned few of them to keep. Diana hated having her picture taken. How had Debra come by this? It was small and looked like it might have been cut from a college yearbook. Of course. Mattie Diamond must have given it to her. Mattie and Diana had been classmates. *Damn her.* He remembered how they had argued about it when Debra was six. Mattie had come to him and said Debra wanted to know about her mother. Josh had forbidden her to talk to the child about the subject, and an awful fight had ensued.

"Find something, Mr. Randall?" Suddenly, Garrigan was at his elbow.

"No."

"Want to tell me about these snapshots?"

"What about them?" Josh didn't know why the man annoyed him so much.

"Who are they? When were they taken?"

Josh identified the people in the snapshots. "I don't see what these have to do with Debra's disappearance."

"I don't know either," Garrigan replied. "I thought maybe you would tell me."

"What do you mean?"

14

"Well, you were certainly studying them. Is there any that were here before that aren't here now?"

Josh shrugged. "I don't know. I never noticed them until now. Look, Garrigan, I only see my daughter occasionally. I'm not that familiar with her things."

"I understand. Just give it a try. There may be something that you know she had, or wore, or cherished. Something that would help us figure out whether she left of her own free will or not."

Josh nodded. "I'll try, but I can't think of anything, offhand."

CHAPTER 4

Paul Diamond felt like an intruder as he opened the closet doors in Debra's bedroom. Everything about the room seemed so personal, almost sacrosanct. From the perfume bottles on the dressing table to the negligee draped across the chair—Debra's essence was everywhere. He had often thought of her in this room—imagined her brushing her silky blond hair, or sleeping, all curled up like a child. He knew just what she would look like, not because she had ever allowed that intimacy he wanted so desperately, but because he knew her better than he knew himself.

Paul moaned and buried his face in the soft silk of one of Debra's blouses. *Oh, God. Deb, where are you?*

He let the memories of the first time he saw her flood his mind. He was five years old when his family moved to the Randall Ranch. He remembered climbing into the cab of the truck to sit between his parents. Daddy had been grim and quiet, and Mama had cried when they left their ranch on the Pecos.

"It's for the best, Mattie," Dad said. "We could never make anything of this place. It's just worn out."

Mama just sat there, her forehead pressed to the window, tears streaming down her face.

"I'd think you'd jump at the chance to live near Diana's baby." His daddy's voice had sounded pleading.

Mama got mad then. She rarely did, but he knew all the signs. Her cheeks turned bright red, and her eyes snapped as if lit by some internal fire.

"It's too late to do anything about what Josh Randall did to Diana, Harry, but I don't think I can stand to sit by and watch him do the same to his daughter."

Daddy had slammed on the brakes so hard it threw Paul into the dashboard. Daddy didn't even notice, just gripped the wheel and gave mama a look that meant he'd had enough. Paul didn't cry. He crouched back into the seat and trembled.

"Mattie, I am sick of your obsession. You have never liked Josh, and you're completely irrational about the subject. Josh never did anything to Diana, except make a damned good living for her. Her place was in LA, where his work is, but because she was homesick, he used money he needed in his business to buy her a ranch on the Rio Grande. How can you..."

"Harry, he crushed her. He never understood her nature. The only thing Josh Randall understands is strength and power. He took her gentleness as weakness, and he tried to punish her for it, tried to change her. Can't you see it?"

"No." Paul remembered his father's voice was low, but it sounded like steel. He put the truck in gear and started up. "I don't want to hear any more about it. Josh is offering me an opportunity to make a life for you and Paul. A good life. I will not have you being ungrateful. Do you understand me?"

He remembered how hard it was not to cry. He hated it when his parents yelled at each other. He couldn't understand it. At five years old, he didn't know who Josh Randall was, but he knew he didn't want to go live with him. He wanted to go home. Meeting Debra had changed that wish, immediately.

17

He'd been asleep when his dad turned into the long, tree-lined lane, but he woke up well before they reached the big white house that sat just below the crest of a hill. He felt a little thrill of anticipation as they pulled up in front. He saw her tiny figure on the porch. At first, he was disappointed to see she was such a little slip of a girl. He stared as she pulled her hand from the lady's grasp and ran down the path. She tripped and sprawled face-down in the gravel. She got up, brushed the dirt and rocks off her knees, and started running again.

"Tough little monkey," Dad had muttered.

He'd thought she would be bigger, but when she threw her pudgy little arms around his middle and smiled up at him, he couldn't resist her. He'd never seen such green eyes.

"Hi," she said. "Are you my new friend?"

They'd been best friends from that day forward.

"Find anything?"

Paul jumped. That damned Garrigan was like a cat. Uncanny that a man his size could move so quietly.

"No. I thought since I saw her every day at the office, I might be able to do best with the clothes." Paul knew he was going to have to concentrate better if he was going to be any help at all.

"Good. If she left on her own, she must have taken some clothes. Do you know her luggage?"

"I don't know," Paul said. "I've seen it, but she might have bought new ones."

"It's in the hall closet. When you finish there, why don't you take a look at it?"

Paul nodded and turned back to the closet.

18

Garrigan asked them all to sit down at the polished mahogany table in the dining room and pulled out his notebook. His fingers strayed to his shirt pocket before he remembered that he had quit smoking a year ago. Funny how the urge still hit him at odd moments.

Josh seemed to have lost some of his hostility and looked gray and drawn. The discovery of the logbook had somehow deflated him. Well, they might as well start with that.

"Were you aware of your daughter's flight to LA in January, Mr. Randall?"

Josh shook his head.

"She didn't go down to see you?"

"I guess not," Josh said. "I didn't see her then. I got no message that she called."

"Diamond?" Garrigan turned to Paul.

"No. I'm trying to remember. What day of the week was that?"

Garrigan consulted the pocket calendar in the back of his notebook.

"Friday."

"A working day," Paul murmured. "I don't remember her taking a day off, but that was over five weeks ago."

Garrigan made a note. "Would you check your personnel records to see if she did?"

"Well, okay. But Debra works out of the office, sometimes, following stories..."

"What was she working on during that period of time?"

Paul shrugged. "I'll look back in our records and find out."

19

"Mallory, do you know anything about that flight?"

"No."

"Where were you at that time?"

Blake reached inside the pocket of his coat, which was hanging on the back of his chair. Leafing through his logbook, he started to hand it to Garrigan.

"Wait a minute. What year is that? Look at the top of the page," Blake said.

"1971, over a year ago," Garrigan muttered, embarrassed that he'd missed that fact. "I didn't notice, as she has filled in the year with ditto marks, and sometimes just the month and day."

Paul asked. "Aren't there more entries on the next page?"

"This is the next to last page. The next one is blank."

"So, she got a new logbook and probably has it with her," Blake added.

"But she didn't take the Rustler," Josh said, a look of alarm on his face.

"We already knew that. She still could have taken another form of transportation," Paul said. "Having her logbook with her doesn't mean anything. I bet she keeps it in her purse."

Garrigan wanted to share Paul's hope, but for some reason, he felt more discouraged. He went on, though.

"Okay, did any of you find anything else missing? What about the luggage, Diamond?"

"Looks like it's all there. But, hell, she could have bought a new set."

"How come you're so damned familiar with her luggage?" Blake asked.

Paul looked at him angrily. "I loaded it in and out of

20

her plane enough times, every fall when she went from Texas to California for school and back."

The two men glared at each other, and Garrigan made another notation in his book.

"You find anything missing, Mr. Randall?"

Josh sighed, a trace of the old exasperation returning to his face.

"Nothing!"

"Clothes?" Garrigan looked at Paul.

Paul, looking miserable, shook his head. "Not that I can think of. But that doesn't mean anything. I almost never saw her except at work. If she decided to take a vacation, she wouldn't take working clothes, would she?"

Garrigan felt compassion for the man's desperate hope. It sure didn't look like Debra Randall had dropped out of sight voluntarily. Still, he couldn't help sharing the young man's desire that she was okay. What was the matter with him anyway? He didn't even know the woman.

"What about jewelry?" he asked.

"I think I can be the authority on that," Josh said. "Debra loved pretty things, but she never, to my knowledge, bought any herself. I gave her jewelry from the time she was nine years old. I looked in the safe in her bedroom. Everything seems to be there."

Garrigan made a note in his book and was about to go on to something else when he noticed Paul Diamond's face. It was ashen.

CHAPTER 5

Paul remembered when he first saw it. Despite his complaints to his buddies that Debra was a pest and a tagalong, Paul was out of sorts on the rare weekends when Josh flew back to the ranch. Suddenly he didn't exist for Deb anymore. It was her tenth birthday, and though they hadn't expected Josh, Paul figured he'd come to surprise her. He watched from a distance as she and Josh rode horseback along the river. He'd felt the rejection keenly. He had taken to spying on them, secure in the knowledge that at the ripe old age of twelve he had mastered the art of stealth and secrecy, and this time was no exception. He realized now that he probably had not fooled Josh for a minute.

After putting his horse away, Paul slipped through the live oak trees near the runway. From the shadows, he watched as Josh leaned down and hugged his little daughter. Her back was ramrod straight, and he knew she would be fighting tears. Josh hated tears. He watched Josh start toward the plane. He was almost there when he heard Debra shout. "You didn't say happy birthday!"

Josh stopped and stood a second before reaching into his pocket and turning back to Debbie. "Fooled you, didn't I," he said with what sounded to Paul like a forced laugh. "I bet you thought I'd forgotten." Paul was too far away to see what he gave her.

Debra stood there long after the plane took off, her fists clenched, watching the sky. Finally, she looked at her present. He could see her shoulders shaking as she walked toward her pony. He knew she would go to their secret place, and he knew she would need him now. He found her lying on the ground, staring at the tops of the cottonwoods through a funny piece of glass.

"Hi," he said.

"Hi."

"Whatcha got?"

"It's a prism," she said proudly.

"Yeah? What's that?"

"Here, I'll show you. You hold it up to the light, then move it just right and you can see all the colors of the rainbow."

She extended the prism and showed him how to move it to make the colors dance.

"That's pretty. Where'd you get it?"

"From Dad."

He'd looked at her, all his annoyance at her desertion melting away at the sight of her woebegone face.

"You been cryin'?"

"Of course not. Why should I be crying over such a neat present, dummy?"

"Yes, you have. I can see the tracks on your face. Is it because he forgot it's your birthday?"

She jumped up angrily, grabbing the prism from his hand.

"Hey, Deb. I'm sorry. Honest. Don't be mad." Touching her he could feel her body shaking. "Deb, it really is a neat prism. Can I see it again? Please."

He had seen it often after that and had come to dread the sight of it. Debra had taken a gold chain from an expensive pendant she never wore and threaded it through the hole drilled in the point of the pyramid. It was about that time she'd started visiting her mother's grave in the little family cemetery on the crest of the hill behind the house. He found her there often, gazing at the prism, her face withdrawn and pale.

He learned to assess her moods by whether or not she wore the prism. The year she was a senior in high school, she hadn't worn it as often, and although he was away at Stanford a good deal of the time, each time he came home, she was the happy, effervescent Debra he had always adored. He had been so proud when she told him she had been named valedictorian, and chatted happily about what a wonderful surprise it would be for her father. He remembered when two days before graduation a package arrived.

They were sitting on the big front porch when it was delivered. Debra opened it and removed a black velvet box. Inside was a pearl necklace and a little white card. He noticed she hardly looked at the necklace and picked up the card with trembling fingers. She didn't say a word as she passed the note to him.

Deb, Honey, Happy Graduation. I hope to make the ceremony, but in case I don't, I wanted you to have this."
Love, Dad"

When Paul drove her to the high school on graduation night, he noticed that the only adornment she wore was the prism necklace. Josh did make the graduation—late. Too late to hear her valedictory speech and see her receive her diploma and awards. He saw she was not wearing the pearls he sent, so again he improvised to appease her. He gave her an airplane.

24

Deb continued to wear the prism. A few weeks later, Josh invited her to come to Los Angeles to live with him, since she planned to attend UCLA in September anyway. She had been ecstatic.

"Oh, Paul. It's going to be so perfect," she'd said, beaming. "I'll miss you, of course, but then I've kind of got used to you being away."

"I'll miss you too, Deb. Somehow, I just can't picture you cooped up in Los Angeles. You're such a free spirit you just sort of belong here," he said, sweeping his arm to include the whole prairie.

"Nonsense. I belong anywhere—and everywhere. There's a whole world out there just waiting for me to claim it."

"What about Blake Mallory? You've been seeing a lot of him, I notice."

Debra looked at him sharply. Did she sense the jealousy he felt?

"Well, I have to admit I'll miss Blake. I'm thinking of trying to get Dad to offer him a job. He knows everything about airplanes."

Was she deliberately teasing? When she looked at him, her green eyes sparkled with mischief. God, she was lovely, but such a child, still.

When he just stared, she asked. "Do you think I'm beautiful, Paul?"

"I think you're a brat!" His face burned.

"Two years at Stanford, and you still blush. I can't believe it. What would your fraternity brothers say?"

His embarrassment turned to anger. Lifting her in his arms, he carried her toward the stock-watering tank.

"No. Paul, please. I'm sorry. No! Don't! Dang you,

Paul Diamond—"

Paul remembered with deep regret that he hadn't listened, but submerged her completely and walked away as she came up sputtering and choking. The remorse and confusion he'd felt that day came back vividly.

He'd mounted his horse and wondered what the hell was the matter with him. He turned toward the river and their "secret place," aching with concern as he thought of the spells that had plagued her the past few years. And he'd just caused one. She found him in the grove of trees.

"Paul?" Her voice was tiny, like a little girl's. "Paul, look at me, please."

Her face was pale, her eyes blurred with pain. He'd grabbed her hand and asked, "Deb, are you all right? You had one of your feelings, didn't you?"

She nodded, her lips pressed tightly together. He could feel her shaking. He helped her to the ground, knowing she wouldn't be able to speak for a while as she dealt with the aftermath. He stroked her forehead and felt the old fear returning. Finally, her mouth began to soften and a little color returned. He lifted her head into his lap.

"How long has this been going on? You told me in your letter they had stopped."

"They did, Paul. Honest. This is the first one in a couple of months."

He doubted that, but didn't argue. Looking down he saw the gold chain disappear into her blouse. He pulled it out, and the prism caught the light. Debra winced, and he covered the glass with his hand.

"Still wearing that thing, huh? I never could understand your fascination for that prism."

Debra pulled it out of his hand and tucked it back inside her shirt.

She started to rise, but he put his hand on her shoulder. "Just lie here for a minute, Kitten. Are you cold? Let me give you my shirt. Your head hurts, doesn't it?"

She nodded slightly, but otherwise ignored the question, her eyes closed.

"What caused the feeling to come on so hard? It was me being jealous, wasn't it?"

"It was the water. You know I have a weird water phobia." Her tone was accusatory.

"I'm so sorry, Kitten. I didn't realize how bad it was, the water, I mean... I didn't think. And, I'm sorry if I sounded jealous."

"Are you, Paul? Is that why you don't like Blake?"

"I guess." Actually, he knew it was. He loved her so much he couldn't stand the thought of anyone else loving her...being intimate in a way he knew he never would be. He sighed and said what was also true. "I just don't want any guy taking advantage of your trusting nature. That's all."

"Good to know you're looking out for me." Her smile melted his heart. "Next time, though, how about throwing the guy in the water instead of me."

"My God, Debra. You're perfect. Just make sure you don't trust anyone who's not worthy of you. Which, by the way, means every man on earth."

CHAPTER 6

"Mr. Diamond?" Garrigan asked. "Did you have something to say?"

Paul shook his head to bring himself back to the present. He noticed that Josh and Blake were watching him quizzically. He wondered how much he'd missed while reminiscing. "No. Nothing."

Garrigan made another notation in his book and studied the gray-faced man.

"Well, we all seem to be tired. Perhaps after each of you have had a chance to think about it, you will come up with something. He solemnly distributed his card to each of the men around the table. "If you think of anything—no matter how trivial it may seem, call me."

Garrigan pushed back his chair and stood up wearily. They rode down the elevator in silence, each man immersed in whatever memories Debra Randall's apartment had evoked. Three men sharing a common agony—yet distant and remote from each other. He sighed.

Garrigan sat in his car for several minutes before starting it, watching the others disperse. Josh Randall got into the Lincoln Continental, which appeared at the curb at some magic signal from the doorman. Paul Diamond shook Josh's hand briefly, before trudging down the sidewalk to the gray sedan parked a few feet from Garrigan's car. Blake Mallory turned up the collar of his coat and stood looking back at the building for several minutes before turning on his heel and striding down Jones

Street, his head bowed, his hands in his coat pocket.

There was a chill in the air and a light drizzle. Garrigan considered offering Blake a lift as he pulled into the street, but something in the young man's manner caused him to change his mind. He waved as he passed him, but Mallory didn't notice. He drove through the streets of the city, deep in thought. He remembered how much he had loved San Francisco when he was younger. He didn't anymore—it had changed somehow, or maybe *he* had. *A sign of old age,* he thought wearily, remembering how his father used to bemoan the changes in his hometown, back in Iowa. "The world's goin' to hell in a handbasket," he used to say. Garrigan hadn't understood that attitude then, but he was beginning to now. He hesitated only briefly before the police station. The hell with it. He needed to think, and the best place for that was at home.

He unlocked the door to his modest little house on Van Ness. He had been told that the house was in the heart of Old German Town, but he didn't know for sure. In a city so rich with history, Pat Garrigan was remarkably oblivious to it. He had moved into the house with his bride in 1945 after he had been discharged from the Navy with a handshake and a Purple Heart. He had loved the house when Mary was alive. She had been a good woman, adapting to his precarious profession with a calm, steadfast faith in his immortality. As he rose through the ranks, they had settled into comfortable acceptance of their life and their childless state. This placid, secure existence had been shattered one day in 1968, when a doped-up kid in a car had plowed into her as she crossed the street. He stopped loving the house after that but just hadn't got around to moving somewhere else.

He hung up his coat and went to the refrigerator for a beer. He turned on the television and went back into the kitchen. He never watched TV, but he needed the sound in the silent, empty house.

Sitting at the kitchen table, Pat took out his notebook and read his notes. Nothing missing—except, possibly, a purse and her current log book. Still, it hadn't been a wasted evening. He didn't know quite what he had learned, except that none of the three men he had met were leveling with him. Turning to a clean sheet he wrote:

Josh Randall: Pocketed the little picture of unknown lady. Check police inventory to see if we have further information about this photo.

Blake Mallory: Visibly upset when he discovered a manuscript. Check tomorrow to see if it's still there. (Bet my next month's pay it isn't.)

Paul Diamond: He thought of something. I don't know what—we were discussing jewelry. Wait a few days, then put the pressure on.

Rereading his notes, Pat made a few more notations. He should eat something, he thought. Shrugging, he got another beer, turned out the lights and sat, unseeing, before the out-of-focus television set. He loosened his tie and closed his eyes. *Where are you, Debra Randall?*

CHAPTER 7

"Where to, sir? The airport?" The chauffeur caught Josh Randall's eyes in the rear-view mirror.

Josh nodded, leaned back against the leather seat, and closed his eyes.

Eddie Miller had driven for Josh for ten years now. He had never seen him look so old and tired. He sighed sympathetically. Like most of Randall's employees, Miller was absolutely devoted to the man. Josh Randall was irascible sometimes, but he was fair. Besides, he drove himself harder than anyone else. Eddie had wanted to be a test pilot for Randall Aircraft. He was twenty-two when he applied. Josh went up with him twice and put him through every maneuver in the book. After the second flight, Josh told him he just didn't have what it took. He'd been furious and hurt. Josh had made no move to stop him when he stalked away. When he reached his car, he noticed that Randall was watching him. Fighting back his rage, he retraced his steps.

"Why?" he demanded, "I have to know why."

Josh had smiled, then, for the first time since Eddie had met him.

"Come in and have a beer, son, and I'll tell you."

He had explained that Eddie was technically a good pilot, but he just didn't have the "gift" Josh required in a test pilot.

"It's something you can't learn. A feeling, a sense of the aircraft, of knowing what every little sound, every little shudder means—the feel of the air, the oil, every little

31

nut and bolt. You either have it, or you don't. You don't. I'm sorry."

Miller accepted that. He knew it was true. What he didn't know then was that anyone could have that "gift."

Now he believed Josh most certainly did. So did Ann, Josh's new bride; and so did Debra. At least he thought she did. Josh wouldn't admit it and wouldn't let her test fly his latest airplanes, but Eddie had a feeling she had it to a greater degree than any of them.

He glanced in the rear-view mirror again. Josh was looking out the window, tapping his teeth with his knuckles.

Garrigan's questions played over and over in Josh's mind. He felt as if he had flunked an important examination, and the sense of failure was unsettling. Garrigan must have sensed how little he knew his daughter. My God, he probably knew more about each of his employees than he knew about Debra. How in the hell had that happened?

He'd been keenly disappointed when she was born. It had never occurred to him that she would be a girl. He had just opened the Randall Aircraft in a rundown warehouse in Orange County. When Diana told him she was pregnant, he had been thrilled. He had even gone out and had a sign designed: RANDALL AND SON. Fortunately, he'd had the good sense not to show it to anyone.

Diana had known how he felt. She had squeezed his hand and told him the next one would be a boy. He guessed she meant it—the doctor hadn't told her yet that she must never have another child.

It wasn't really until Debra came to live with him while she went to UCLA that he really got to know her.

She had worked at the plant part-time, and he'd been impressed with her competence. Those first three years she went to college had probably been the best they'd ever had. When he met Ann and gave her the job to test the Ranger, he knew Deb had been deeply hurt. It wasn't until he told Deb they were getting married that the real rift developed.

Strangely, Debra and Ann had become good friends, but the coolness between Debra and him had only grown.

Josh reached inside his jacket and pulled out the tiny, framed picture of Diana. Switching on the reading light, he studied the photo. He realized that his image of Diana had been replaced with Debra's features. Deb looked like her, but she had more substance. Diana was so fragile, and even at eighteen, as she must have been in this picture, something of the awful thing that was to destroy her was evident. He had long ago conquered the pain, but it wasn't until now that he realized he had replaced it with hatred. Was that why he had held back his full love from his daughter? Poor Debra. *I couldn't let you know your mother, but I should have at least given you a father.* The tightening in his chest was more than remorse, it was fear. That senseless, shameful fear he had felt before Diana died. Fear of something he couldn't understand.

He snapped off the light and leaned back. *I've got to find her. I've got to find her and explain. I can't live with hurting her like I hurt her mother.*

"Mr. Randall?" Eddie's voice brought him back to the present. He stepped out of the open door and walked toward the small airplane that would take him home to Ann.

33

CHAPTER 8

Paul Diamond maneuvered his car through the streets of San Francisco by pure habit. He lit a cigarette with shaking fingers and tried to separate his thought from the emotions that had churned through him at Debra's apartment.

He pulled into the tree-lined drive leading to his house and doused the lights. Easing toward the garage, he shut off the ignition. He needed some time alone. Besides, he was in no hurry to go inside and face Maureen's accusations of neglect. She would never understand. She'd never liked Debra and had always been jealous. When Deb first disappeared, she feigned concern, but had done little to hide her elation. If Garrigan ever questioned her, he would probably think she was a prime suspect.

Garrigan was good. Josh might consider him a bumbler, but Paul had known enough detectives to know he was sharp. *He doesn't seem to be very close to solving the mystery, though,* Paul thought bitterly.

Oh, God, Debra, where are you? Are you all right? You must know I'm worried sick. Paul put his face in his hands and fought the rising panic. Why hadn't he told Garrigan about the prism? The fact that it wasn't there, really didn't mean anything, except that she was probably wearing it—and that probably meant she was unhappy and possibly sick again. *I've got to tell him about the illness,* he thought. *Surely, she wouldn't expect me to keep my promise in a case like this—not when it might save her life.*

He remembered her face when she had finally agreed to talk about it. So white, her eyes so big, so frightened. "It's so hard to describe, Paul. It's like something takes possession of my body, and I just go away for a while."

"Can you feel them coming, baby?"

"Sort of, but that's no help. I can't do a thing. I hear this music, kind of soft and far away, then it builds and builds into a crescendo kind of like a waterfall, drowning out everything—then...Oh, you're going to think I'm crazy...."

"Debra, you're not crazy. I want to hear this, all of it. I don't care how you think it sounds."

"Well," she averted her eyes and played with the prism. "Then I hear this voice. It's a woman's voice, very soft, very far away, calling my name."

"Then what?"

"Then I start to feel the pain—in my head—and realize where I am, what I'm doing, but with no sense of how long I was gone, or what I did. I feel sick—sometimes I throw up. Then I have a headache for a couple of hours, and I'm me again."

"What does the doctor say?"

She looked away, her eyes closed, her jaw tight.

"Debra?"

"Nothing. I've had all the tests, the brain scan, the EEG, the spinal tap, the works...He says I'm perfectly normal!"

"Then go to another doctor. Obviously, he's wrong."

"He told me I should see a psychiatrist." Her voice was trembling, her eyes filled with tears.

"So, why don't you?"

"You, too!" She'd jumped up and paced the floor, her

eyes flashing behind the tears. "You think I'm nuts!"

He grabbed her shoulders, shook her gently, and then hugged her to his chest.

"Debra, you're the last person in the world I would think was nuts. But, Kitten, maybe there is some sort of stress you're expressing, or holding in, or something. It's worth a shot. You could at least talk to a shrink. Or better still, a neurologist. Please, Debra, we've got to find out what's causing these things."

She had promised she would see someone, but he didn't think she ever had. And she had made him promise not to say anything to Josh or anyone. Like a fool, he hadn't—and now she had disappeared.

He sighed and reached for the door handle. With one glance at the lighted window he sat back and tapped out another cigarette. He just wasn't ready to face his wife. Not on top of all the other agony he was going through.

He remembered when he'd first met Maureen. It had been at Josh Randall's wedding. Deb had begged him to be her escort of the day. Well, "protector" is the word she'd used. He was eager of course to sit with her, dance with her, just to be by her side.

"I thought your boyfriend was coming," he prompted, wondering what had happened to that plan. The only explanation she offered was, "He couldn't make it."

The look on her face let him know there was much more to the story than that, but he knew not to push.

Debra had not been happy about her father's marriage. Paul thought it was typical of Josh's insensitivity that he hadn't even told Deb he was dating before springing the news of the engagement on her. The casual way he'd told her that Ann, his bride, was the test pilot for the new plane in the Andean Sierras, a job she'd begged her dad for, nearly broke her heart.

She'd clung to Paul's hand with a death grip all through the ceremony and wanted to leave as soon as it was over. They were discussing it when Ann was getting ready to toss the bouquet. He urged her to catch it.

"No, thanks," she'd said, backing away. A tall, shapely redhead reached in front of her and caught it. She turned to look at Debra, then Paul, and smiled.

"I hope you weren't going for this." With her face buried to her nose in the flowers and her hair gleaming like a new penny in the sunlight, she batted her long-lashed, blue eyes at Paul.

"I'm sure Paul had no interest in catching the bouquet," Debra had said, clutching Paul's arm.

The woman giggled. "Not him. I meant you, of course."

"Oh, silly me. I could have sworn you were looking at him."

"Look!" the stranger shouted, grasping Paul's forearm, "Josh is tossing the garter."

Both Debra and Paul looked up in time to see a blue, silk garter sailing through the air at them. Paul snagged it, or it would have hit Debra in the face.

"You caught it," the woman squealed. "Looks like we're both looking at marriage in our future."

"I don't know about that," Paul said. "I had no intention of catching this. I didn't have time to think."

"All the more proof it was meant for you." The woman winked, her heavily accentuated blue eyes sparkling. "Forgive my manners. I'm Maureen, Ann's cousin. She was radiant today, don't you think?"

"Indeed," Paul said, as he stared at Maureen. "I'm Paul Diamond, and this is my friend, Debra Randall, the daughter of the groom."

"I'm so pleased to meet you," Maureen said, offering her hand to Paul. "To meet you both on this gorgeous spring day. We're Irish, you know, and so what better day to get married than on St. Patrick's Day?" She glanced at Debra, "This must be a happy day for you, seeing your father make such a good catch."

Debra glared. "I think it's your cousin who made the great catch, don't you?"

Had he sensed the strength of Debra's jealousy at the time? Of course he had, and he'd exploited it. If Debra was that jealous and protective, it meant she cared.

He sighed and lit another cigarette. He remembered Deb's plaintive voice

"Paul, I'd like to go now."

"Sure," he'd said. "Very nice to meet you Maureen," and he walked Debra to his rental car and held the door for her. "Are you feeling all right, Kitten?" he asked.

"Yeah. I'm fine. Kind of exhausted, I guess." Debra didn't admit to the emotions raging in her. Paul knew her well enough to know she was steaming at the way he'd looked at Maureen. He'd felt guilty and offered to take her home and stay with her until she felt better. He hoped she'd agree and was surprised when she said, "No, I just need some time alone, I think." Her anger seemed to vanish into exhaustion.

"You sure? I don't think you're feeling well."

"Nothing some air time won't cure." Debra squeezed his arm. "It's the best medicine there is for jangled nerves, and believe me, this day has jangled my nerves."

"Do you think you should be flying? The stress you've been under with this wedding is the kind of thing that can bring on one of your feelings."

She always insisted on calling the strange spells that overtook her at times, "feelings." A doctor once told her they were not seizures, and Paul hated the doctor for it. But Debra refused to get a second opinion, declaring, "It's just a weird feeling I get that grows into something I can't describe, but it's just in my head, according to the doctor."

She didn't know what caused them any more than Paul did, but he worried that the stress of this day could bring one on.

"Do you want to come with me?" she asked.

"You know I'd love to, Kitten, but Dad will be looking for me. He feels like a fish out of water in this town. I imagine he's beginning to panic already." If Paul's mother had come, he wouldn't have felt so responsible for Harry.

Debra had sighed. "I understand, and don't worry. I'm not going to have one of my feelings. I never do when I'm flying. I've told you that."

"There's a first time for everything," he muttered, an argument she ignored.

At Randall's airfield, Debra gave Paul a hug and a kiss on the cheek. "Enjoy the rest of your day, Pablito. And thanks for everything."

Paul smiled at her use of her pet name for him. She'd been calling him the Spanish name for "little Paul" since she heard his mother use it once in early childhood. It must mean she wasn't mad at him. He sighed and went back to the reception where Maureen immediately found him and asked him to dance.

Two days later, Paul helped Debra move her belongings to the dorm. She wanted to be long gone by the time Josh and Ann returned from their honeymoon in the Bahamas. It was difficult to fit everything from her large bedroom, attached bath, and private office into half of even the newest, most spacious dormitory room. She'd wanted a private room, but none was available. When the last box was carried up the long flight of stairs and stowed under her bed, Paul pulled Debra into a hug and kissed her on the forehead.

"There you go, Kitten. I hope you like it here. Call me when you're ready to move out."

"I was hoping we could go get a bite to eat, Paul," Debra said, as he headed for the door.

He remembered the sudden twinge of guilt, and for the first time in his life, considered standing up a date. He remembered his stammered reply, "Oh, I'd love to, Kitten, but...um, actually I have plans. I'm a little late as it is."

"A date? I didn't know you knew anyone in LA."

"Uh, I'm taking Maureen to a dinner theater. She asked me, actually."

"Oh, I see. I guess you'd better go, then."

"You're not mad that I accepted her invitation, are you?" He'd been genuinely concerned, and if Deb would tell him she needed him, he'd leave Maureen standing and do whatever Deb wanted to do, but she'd said, "Of course not. You go and have fun. I'll just get some things put away before my roommate comes back from supper."

And he'd gone, forgetting Deb while Maureen turned

on her charms. He'd been surprised by how easily he slipped into her bed that night and how sensually thrilling it had been.

Funny how one of the most exciting times of your life could lead to the most miserable. And that's how he'd felt when he married Maureen several months later. The feeling of doom he felt, standing in front of the church watching the glamorous woman advance ominously toward him on her father's well-muscled arm, made him want to run. He was doomed, and to make it worse, his best friend, the girl he loved more than life, had not shown up.

Tears welled in his eyes, and not for the smoke that filled the car. He looked at the cigarette between his fingers and wondered how many he'd smoked.

A pounding on the window jarred him out of his reverie.

"What the hell are you doing?" Maureen demanded. "I've been pacing the floor for hours and was ready to call the cops when I looked out the door and saw the glow of your cigarette."

She pounded again, and he rolled the window down. It had been cracked enough to let the smoke roll out but not enough to let the rain in.

"I thought you'd been killed in some traffic accident or shot by a crazy drunk or something. Have you no idea how much worry and stress you caused me? You don't care, do you? You selfish son of a bitch!"

Paul tried to interrupt the tirade, but Maureen was going full steam.

"All you think of is yourself and your old girlfriend,

because you can't accept that she is gone. Gone, Paul! It's time you realize you have a wife who needs you. Now get the hell out of the car and come in the house where you belong, so I can get out of this damned rain."

Every inkling of guilt Paul had been feeling vanished with the mention of Debra. He was a gentle soul and rarely got angry, but he was angry now.

"No, Maureen. You go back inside. Go to bed. I have to go to the *Examiner* and copy some files for Garrigan."

"What? You're leaving? At this time of night?"

"I am. I'll see you in the morning."

Maureen grabbed the door handle and tried to wrench it open, but it was locked, and the car was inching backward.

Maureen let go, stooped to pick up a rock, and hurled it at her husband. It bounced off the driver's side window and back into the driveway. When he turned and started up the street, he looked back to see Maureen hugging herself and crying.

Quelling the urge to go back and comfort her, he kept going.

CHAPTER 9

Jamming his hands deep into the pockets of his sheep skin-lined coat, Blake Mallory walked through the foggy streets. He was well aware that Garrigan was watching him from his car. *Let him watch*, he thought bitterly. *If he suspects I know where Debra is, he's really on the wrong track.* .

Now, with the discovery of the manuscript, he was less hopeful that Debra had left on her own, that she was okay. They hadn't heard from his brother, Kent, for over a year and a half, since their Canadian encounter. No doubt, though, he was probably still involved in his drug operation. He feared that Debra had grown too complacent after not hearing from him for so long. Oh, hell. Maybe she had heard from him. Maybe she'd gotten enough sinister threats that she felt she had to hide? She wouldn't tell him after their breakup, would she?

When veiled warnings addressed to Debra arrived at the newspaper office, letting them know Kent was alive and stalking her, Blake had begun plotting to eliminate his brother. He knew of no other way to stop him. He couldn't trust the cops. They'd nearly lost their lives learning that Kent owned the cops, and they didn't know how far his reach extended. Maybe he should sound out his mother first. He never had determined how much she was involved in Kent's operation.

Funny what concentric coincidences life held. For years he'd looked for his mother—only to find her through Debra. Could it be that hope of discovering

43

Debra's fate might lie with Ellen Wainwright?

Blake was jolted out of his reverie by the blast of a horn. He had stepped into the street without looking and a big black car swerved to avoid him, the driver shook his fist and yelled something obscene.

Blake crossed the street, stopped under an awning, and glared as the red dots of the taillights disappeared into the fog. He hated California. He remembered the first time he had seen it—drawn by Debra's pleas. It was the April of her father's wedding, and he had finally agreed to fly out for a weekend to give her support.

Debra had insisted on taking him to meet a friend of hers, even though he'd much rather have spent every minute with her. How surprised he'd been to come face to face with his mother, who now called herself Ellen Wainwright. No wonder he'd never been able to find her through all his years of searching. He hadn't even known her maiden name when he was growing up. People outside the family just called her Mrs. Mallory.

Debra had been just as surprised. And Ellen seemed overwhelmed—all tears and she couldn't stop talking. They'd gone to her place when she got off work and talked long into the night about the twelve years that had passed since she'd left her sons with their drunken father.

Finally, Ellen had taken both of them into her confidence and told them about the work she was doing to help young men dodge the draft. If only someone could fly them across the border, it would help so much. Blake refused, but Debra immediately volunteered. A terrible fight had ensued, ending in their first breakup. Finally, though, because of his feelings for Debra, he agreed to help. When he did, much to everyone's surprise, he discovered his brother, a man he had never wished to see again. It wasn't a happy reunion. Nor would the next one be. Blake was ready to give his life if it would save Debra.

The fog was really socking in now. What an awful place. Well, there was nothing to do but fly to LA and see his mother. She didn't know where Debra was, he'd already checked. But she probably knew where Kent was, for he had a sickening feeling that his mother was more involved with Kent than she let on.

He glanced at the hotel where the doorman, holding an umbrella, escorted a couple from their car to the canopy over the door. He jogged across the street and the half block to the hotel. As the couple entered, he said to the doorman, "I dropped my keys in there," and followed the couple inside.

Patrick Garrigan arrived at his office early. The streets were still fog-bound and nearly deserted. The desk sergeant nodded sleepily. He had long ago ceased wondering why Garrigan appeared at the station at such odd hours.

Pat poured himself a cup of the black coffee and closed his office door. On his desk was a thick, manila envelope with the logo of the *Examiner* printed on the corner. Paul Diamond had kept his word and had it delivered sometime in the night. Pat opened it and shook the contents onto his scarred, wooden desk. He noted absently that they were photocopies of the original clippings and wondered if Paul himself had stood at the copier after last night's session.

He wished Randall and Mallory were as cooperative.

The pages had been collated chronologically, with the most recent on top. It was dated just a month ago, and showed a serene and solemn Debra Randall talking to the newly elected governor. Pat scanned the article, and then studied her picture. Her blond hair was pulled back into a bun, accentuating her high cheekbones and large eyes. The article was well written and subtly reflected the *Examiner's* support of the conservative governor. It revealed absolutely nothing about the writer, other than her obvious mastery of her craft. He turned the page.

Pat stretched and reached for his coffee. It was cold. He started reading the next article.

CHAPTER 10

Having learned nothing conclusive from his mother, Blake returned to his small airport in Marfa, Texas. Before going to bed, he wondered what he should do with the manuscript he'd taken from Debra's apartment. *Burn it,* he thought. *What good can come from anyone reading it?* Aiding and abetting draft dodgers, helping them leave the country to escape serving was a federal offense. He didn't know what the maximum penalty was, but he didn't relish the idea of visiting his girlfriend in prison. Perhaps, though, the manuscript could be used as evidence against Kent. But, no. Kent won't be alive to face trial. *Unless he kills me first.* Blake was determined that wouldn't happen.

Well, he would read it first. Maybe something in it would help him find her.

CANADIAN ODYSSEY
by
D. Randall

Blake noticed a handwritten note on the back of the title page before the beginning of the first chapter. It said:

> To whomever finds this when I'm gone:
> I started this account of what happened in Canada as a novel, but quickly decided, after a few false starts, that I'm a journalist, not a novelist. I'll quit trying to keep track of fake names and places and just record a true account, like a

diary. If anyone comes along later and wants to turn it into a book, be my guest. After I record the secret, horrific past events, I'll keep making journal entries as life unfolds.

Los Angeles, California: June 18, 1970

The early morning mission began like all the others at the meeting in Ellen's kitchen with young men desperate to escape the lottery they'd just won. Prize: the chance to sacrifice their lives in a war they did not believe in, taking place in a jungle they never wanted to see. They'd rather risk imprisonment. That's where I come in, willing to take the chance right along with them. Ellen, a friend and mother figure to me, was the boys' link to safety. I provided the vehicle.

Unlike other mornings, there were more passengers, the weather was terrible, but what really made this flight special was having a co-pilot.

When Blake, my boyfriend, agreed to come on board, my heart melted. We'd broken up three months earlier over an argument we had after I agreed to join this illegal operation and important cause with his mother.

I was as shocked as he was when I introduced him to Ellen and discovered that she was his long-lost mother. Of course, I had no idea they were related when I first met Ellen. Always a sucker for sad eyes, I had been immediately disarmed by the woman who stopped to check on me when I had to pull off the street to nurse a headache. Now I notice Blake has the same startling, deep blue eyes. Both his and his mother's are gorgeous—and mysterious.

As an undergraduate looking for a story, I saw one in this sad, empathic woman. The angel of Skid Row, Los Angeles, worked in a hole-in-the-wall restaurant on a dirty street inhabited by the down and out. I learned that it was compassion that fueled the sadness—a deep sorrow that she could never do enough to help the young men the government sought to exploit.

When Ellen asked Blake to help, he refused and I volunteered. Our relationship ended that day.

Blake closed his eyes and sat with his face cradled in his hands. *You're leaving out the facts of the matter, Debra.* He remembered the shock he felt at Debra's anger. It had made no sense. She'd driven like a maniac through the streets of LA just because he'd refused to jump at the chance to take part in the smuggling operation of the woman who'd deserted him when he was a child. Or maybe it was a remark he'd made about Debra's ability as a pilot. He hadn't meant it. He'd only answered, "That, too," when she asked if he didn't think she was capable of flying across the border.

But when he apologized, she just told him to get out, and to get out *NOW*. He'd slammed the car door and strode away, so hurt and angry he never looked back. Her reaction made no sense. What did she expect after introducing him to his mother, a woman who'd walked out of his life him ten years ago, leaving him with a drunken father and brother?

49

When she ordered him out of her car—and out of her life—she was quivering with anger. She wouldn't let him explain. It was like she couldn't wait to get rid of him—like she thought he'd hurt her, but that made no sense.

At the time, Blake wished he'd never gone to California. He was supposed to help her get through her Dad's wedding. They couldn't even get through meeting his mom.

He'd vowed to forget Debra Randall. But forgetting proved to be impossible. Images of her would streak across his mind at the least expected moment. He kept busy, but memories of her laughing green eyes challenged him while he worked on airplanes. Visions of her shapely figure and smooth skin tantalized him in dreams. Memories of her laughter, her sweetness, brought him to tears when he rose from the runway and banked over the Texas prairie. His heart felt like it was breaking when he looked down on the Randall Ranch, sure he'd never see her again.

Blake picked up the manuscript and read on.

> The rain-wet streets of the city seemed to absorb all light, making the predawn hour darker than the darkest midnight. Ellen asked if we wanted to postpone. "The weather calls for high winds and more rain," she warned.
>
> Not one of the six young men with orders to report for the draft wanted to wait.
>
> "I want to be in another country before the draft office opens today," one young man said. The other five agreed.
>
> "Is it safe?" Ellen asked.

"Sure," I answered. "I've flown in worse. It'll just make it easier to sneak out the Raptor." I had permission to borrow Dad's new six passenger turbo prop, but he hadn't said when—and of course, he didn't know why.

I looked at Blake for confirmation. When he nodded and said, "No problem," my heart exploded with joy.

Oh, Debra, where are you? Would it have saved you, if I'd said, 'no?' Tears clouded Blake's eyes, and he put the manuscript down. How he wished he could hold her instead of a ream of paper. He wished he'd done more to protect her. Feeling sure she was either dead or a tortured captive, he cursed himself and sobbed until sleep finally claimed him.

CHAPTER 11

Blake was jolted awake from a nightmare in which his brother leaned over Debra's chained body, holding a knife to her throat. Blake tried to save her, but found his arms and legs bolted to a concrete wall.

Sweating and jittery, he got up and began pacing. The dream was right out of Kent's morbid plan, which he'd laid out in graphic detail as he held them both prisoners. It could be happening to Debra right now.

Blake punched the wall—hard—to ward off another surge of unwelcome tears. He prepared coffee and put it on the hot plate to perk.

Picking up the manuscript from the floor beside the couch he read:

> I started flying for Ellen, taking young men to Canada, a few days after Dad's wedding on St. Patrick's Day that year. I'd already made several flights to Kelowna by the end of May, when my graduation from UCLA loomed. I told Ellen, "I can't fly next weekend because of graduation, then I'm going back to the ranch in Texas for a few days."
>
> "I understand," Ellen said—not looking happy. "Come talk to me when you get back. Maybe we can work out a new schedule for summer."
>
> "Yeah. I'll come talk about it. I might be getting a job in San Francisco, so I don't know for sure." When I saw a flash of disappointment on Ellen's face, I added, "I won't be working weekends, so I'll still help." And just like that I

decided to keep flying boys to Canada.

Graduation meant many changes in my life. I'd worked for Randall Aircraft for four years and loved it. I lived on my own since my father's April wedding. After graduation, I didn't go back to work there. I turned in my letter of resignation two weeks earlier.

Dad had said, "Hey, you don't have to be so formal."

"Why not?" I asked. "This has been a real job. You'd expect as much from any of your other employees."

Then he got all angry and said, "What is this I hear about you working in a dive in the seedy side of town? Is that what you intend to do with your education?"

"No. I went there to get a story, one I got a good grade on, by the way. It was temporary. I plan to go to San Francisco and work for the Examiner."

I guessed that's what I'd do, eventually at least, but first I wanted to continue to fly young men to Canada. I truly believed it was my calling. Nothing excited me like knowing I was saving lives the government intended to sacrifice. I also wanted to keep writing about the war and what it does to the teenage boys who did not escape the draft, to their families, and to the country.

When I addressed graduation announcements, I deliberately left Blake out. But later, as I thought about how cruelly I'd kicked him out, I decided to give him—and our relationship—another chance. At the very least, I owed him an apology. And, I didn't know if there was a chance for a relationship, but if there was even a slight possibility for reconciliation, I owed it to him—and to myself, to take it. Because I'd found I could not forget him. I knew I had to tell him everything, and he'd have to accept me as I am, and that includes my "feelings." It was a lot to expect, but I would never know if I didn't ask. I pulled out an invitation and wrote.

Dear Blake,

Please come to my party at the ranch. It will be much more fun than the graduation which will be long, boring, and stuffy with thousands of people present.

I understand if you're still mad at me for the way I treated you the last time I saw you. I don't blame you, but I'm asking you to accept my apology. If you come to the party, I'll know you are willing to give me a chance to explain. I want to.

Humbly yours,

Debra

My heartbeat quickened when I sealed it, but then I let it hover over the waste basket while I tried to screw up my courage. Did I really want to do this? I thought of Blake. There is something about him, an air of self-reliance, quiet strength, and unwavering honesty that makes every other man I meet pale by comparison. Would he give me another chance? If he refused to take me back, I'd have to try harder to forget him. Instead of dropping the invitation in the waste basket, I put it in the mail.

Blake put down the diary as memories of their breakup flooded over him. What haunted him most was the look on her face, pain—and something else—when she told him to leave. It looked like panic. Sure, she'd been angry, but that didn't explain what was going on behind those imploring green eyes. That's why he couldn't resist her invitation.

He'd flown to the Randall Ranch early, hoping to be the first to arrive at the party. As he approached Randall's private landing strip, he saw Debra running down the path from the house to meet him. He taxied to a stop at the end of the runway, and there she was, eager anticipation on her beautiful face as he stepped from the plane. Their conversation was locked in his mind.

"Hi. I was afraid you wouldn't come," she'd said.

"I'm here," he answered as his heart raced. "I've missed you—and I've been baffled by what happened that day. You said you'd explain."

And she did, or he'd thought so at the time, never suspecting it was only a partial admission.

She took a deep breath, getting up courage, it seemed, for a big confession. "Well, for starters, I'm not sure why I got so angry that day. I think I expected you to be as excited as I was about helping young men—boys, really—escape the travesty of this war. And you weren't. You didn't want to be involved, and then you were pouting because I said I would. I didn't take into account that I'd been thinking about this for a long time, but you had just heard about it."

"And the fact that I didn't jump on board made you so angry you wanted to get rid of me without giving me

a chance to talk about it?" Blake remembered the indig-
nation and the pain that even he'd heard in his voice. "I
couldn't see why you wouldn't at least discuss it before
throwing me out."

It took her a while and a lot of pacing, but she finally
told him she'd felt a spell of some kind coming on that
made her feel funny. She called it a "feeling." And she
knew she'd have an awful headache and get sick before
it was over.

Blake was incredulous. "You thought I couldn't handle seeing you sick? You don't trust me at all, do you?"

"No, it's not like that. I'm the one who couldn't handle
it. I've always had to be alone when one hit me, and this
one was coming on fast."

This is crazy, he remembered thinking, but it did kind
of explain the look in her eyes that day. "Migraines?"
he'd asked.

"Yeah, sort of like that," she said with a lot of hesitation in her voice. "Sort of like really bad migraines."

He'd taken her into his arms and begged her to trust
him. Then he said, "I may not have told you this before,
but I love you. I probably shouldn't. I know I shouldn't,
but I can't help it. I just do. That means, if you'll let me,
I'll be there for you through anything—sickness and
health, as they say."

Her face relaxed, and the tears that had been brim-
ming in her eyes streamed down her face. "Thank you
for saying that. I was hoping you would, and I'll try to
trust you. As I've already said, it's not because of you.
It's me."

Then he'd pulled her closer. "Debra, I've been thinking a lot since that day, and I want apologize for what I

said the last time I saw you. I had no right to doubt you or to tell you what you should do."

"Really?" She squeezed his hand that relaxed warmly in her grasp. "Thank you, Blake. I can easily forgive that, if you can forgive me. I'm glad to know you've been thinking about me."

"Will I be in trouble again if I tell you I can't quit thinking about you—worrying about you?"

"No, not at all, but please don't waste your time worrying. I'm..."

"I know. You're one of the best pilots in the country, but that doesn't keep me from worrying."

She'd tried to reply, but Blake pressed on. "So, I've decided that if the offer is still open, I'll join the cause and fly with you. We can be partners, if you'll let me."

Blake closed his eyes and wished like hell he hadn't offered. Hadn't even gone to her party. If he'd stayed away, she probably would not have gone to Kent's ranch. And she'd still be alive. Maybe. Shit. Too late now to change anything.

He remembered the first—and last—time he'd flown to Canada with her. The one she'd begun describing at the beginning of her manuscript turned journal. When Debra logged her flights to Kelowna, British Columbia, a city known for tourism, no one, not even Josh Randall, questioned why she would go there. In mid-July, she talked her father into letting her fly the Randall Raptor, a six-passenger single engine, turbo prop. She told her dad she wanted to show it off to "her boyfriend," which may have been true, as she'd let him fly to Kelowna, but she also needed the bigger plane for six men who needed to go to Canada, pronto. Josh was proud of this plane, and rightly so. The sleek single engine, turbo-prop was designed to be both fast and fuel-efficient.

Just outside the Kelowna terminal, a tall, slender man, smoking a cigarette, leaned against a VW bus, painted with flowers and graffiti.

"Hi, Sam," Debra called to him as they approach, "I'd like you to meet my new partner, Blake Mallory."

Blake had stopped, stunned. Sam's jaw dropped; his eyes widened. Blake watched his brother's perpetual smirk slowly reappear.

"Well, I'll be damned," Sam said. "I never thought Momma would share the business with her little angel."

"Kent?" Blake croaked. "You're Mother's Canadian contact?"

"What? You two know each other?" Debra asked.

"Seems you have a way of finding my long-lost family for me, Deb." Blake put a protective arm around her shoulders.

"Well, this calls for a celebration," Kent crowed. "Squeeze in with the rest of these guys, and I'll take you to my ranch."

"You two are related?" Debra asked looking from one to the other as if searching for similarities.

"You got it," Kent crowed. "Brothers, no less. Come on. We'll have a big dinner, and you can spend the night in style."

"Thanks," Debra said. "We were planning to stay in town, but this sounds even better."

"We're renting a car," Blake said, taking Debra by the elbow. "We'll drive, if you give us the address."

"No need for that. It isn't the easiest place to find. I'll wait, and you can follow."

Blake guided Debra away.

"I'm sorry. I should have asked if you wanted to go. I just assumed..." she began.

"Don't ever assume anything that concerns Kent Mallory," Blake growled. "I have a bad feeling about this."

"We can tell him we decided to stay in Kelowna because we already have a room booked, which we do."

Blake sighed. "I know you've been curious about where your passengers go. You've wanted the chance to check him out, right?"

Debra nodded. "I really do want to see it all with my own eyes, so I know I'm doing the right thing."

"We can come back after we eat."

As they drove, Debra told him of the men she had come to know and care about when she flew them from the grasp of the draft board.

"Most put on the show of bravado and complained about the unfairness of this 'violation of their human rights,' and I agree. But some seemed plain scared, not wanting to leave home, but choosing this over going to the jungle to kill people they don't even know, and though they didn't say it as much, being killed.

"There was this one kid that really got me thinking. He was terrified, and didn't mind admitting it. Skinny and plagued with acne, he didn't have the confident swagger of some of the boys. He looked downright scared.

"I asked if he'd ever flown before, and he said he hadn't.

I tried to reassure him by saying, 'I'm a good pilot,

and this is a reliable plane.'

"To my surprise, he said, 'Oh, I'm not afraid of flying,' so, I asked him more questions, like why he decided to come to Canada, rather than reporting for the draft. I asked if Ellen talked him into it?

"He said, 'Oh, no. It doesn't work that way. We have to convince her that we have a real reason for not wanting to go to war.'

"I asked what he told her, and he gave her the same answer I've heard most of them give. He disagreed with the whole reason our country is in Vietnam. He asked why he should go fight for some little country that has nothing to do with him. He said, 'I don't want to kill people I don't even know.'"

"Good point," Blake said. "Can't blame him there."

"It was the same story I heard from many other young men. Yet each was different in subtle ways." Debra had paused, sighed, and continued. "I sensed vulnerability in this kid. More than usual, I mean. They're all just kids who've won the lottery for a chance to leave everything they know and love to go halfway around the world to a steamy jungle to kill or be killed—or both. Most worked hard not to show their fear.

"I wanted him to tell me more, so I asked his name and where he was from," Debra continued.

"'Jacob Bentley,' he said, 'but you can call me Jake.' He told me he's from Colorado, but he moved to Los Angeles to live with his aunt. He kind of choked up when he said, 'I was going to go to school next fall. But then my number got called up.'

"I told him it was a good thing he met Ellen and that I was sure he'd like British Columbia better than he'd have liked Nam.

"His voice cracked when he asked, 'What's it like?'

"I described it's beauty and told him Canada is sympathetic to those who don't want to fight. They don't agree with our involvement in the war.

"But then he asked, 'What about the guy that's supposed to get us jobs. What's he like?' and I saw his fear was coming from the unknown. I tried to reassure him by describing the guy as young, probably in his mid to late twenties, good looking, charming, and easy to talk to. Jake seemed near tears when he said, 'I don't care about those things. What will he do to help me?'

"I said, 'Well, from what Ellen tells me, he has a ranch or a farm. He hires guys like you to work for him if they want to, and I suppose he helps find some of them other jobs. I doubt he can hire everyone, but at least he gives them a start and a place to stay.' But Jake didn't look satisfied.

"I asked, 'What kind of work do you want to find?'

"He said, 'I just have a really bad feeling about it. I don't know why. Of course, I keep telling myself it will be better than going to the army, but what I really want is a chance to go to school. I want to be a doctor. Not the kind that treats patients, but do research and find a cure for bad diseases.'

"I said, 'I'm sure Canada has good schools. Hopefully, this guy—his name's Sam Smith—will know how to get you into one.'

"But, he kind of stopped me when he asked, 'Do you know that?' and I had to admit I didn't know anything for sure. I asked if he had asked Ellen because she's the one who knows him. He said he did, and she told him to tell this guy what he wanted, and he'd probably get him in touch with the right people.'

"I just said, 'Well, there you go,' But I wasn't sure anymore. So, you see why I want to see your brother's operation. I want to know if he actually helped Jake. I sure hope so, because I can't forget what Jake said next. He chuckled nervously and said, 'It's just this crazy feeling I have. Like impending doom. It's probably nothing, but I can't seem to get over it. I hope I'm all wrong.'" Debra sighed and said, "I hope so, too. I worry about him."

Blake put his hand on her knee, and whispered. "I hope so, too, Deb. I really hope so."

CHAPTER 12

The road was long and winding. About two hours out of town, Kent turned off on a gravel road, and two miles farther, he took a left onto a narrow, dirt lane. It wound through trees for another mile until it ended at a large log house and several outbuildings, including two long Quonset-style greenhouses.

Kent pointed the six young men to the bunkhouse. "Just knock on the door. They'll tell ya where to put your things."

He led Debra and Blake past a fishpond with a fountain into the main house. "Millie," he hollered. "Put on some extra steaks. We have important guests tonight."

A young Asian woman came from the kitchen, wiping her hands on a towel. She smiled and bowed. "Welcome," she said. "Dinner will be ready in twenty minutes."

"Millie, meet my brother, Blake, and Debra, the pilot I've been telling you about."

"Oh, I didn't know you have a brother." Millie's eyes widened. "I'll make sure he gets the best steak." She looked at Debra. "You, too, Miss Airplane Pilot. Sammy tells me how good you fly."

Kent led them back to lawn chairs on the patio.

"Looks like you have quite an operation, here, Kent," Blake said. "How'd you get started?"

"Long story, bro," Kent drawled as he tapped a cigarette from a half empty pack and then offered one to Blake.

Blake shook his head, and Kent continued, "In the

63

morning, I'll show you around, but for now, let's just say I was lucky to hit the jackpot when I decided to move north instead of checking out the jungles of Vietnam."

"What do you grow in the greenhouses?" Debra asked.

He squinted as he lit his cigarette, inhaled deeply, and blew out a long puff of smoke. "That's where we start our plants, mostly vegetables and flowers. Sell them in a little store in Kelowna."

"Do you raise cattle?" Blake asked.

"Yeah, sure. You'll be eating some of it tonight."

"I'm impressed," Debra said. "No wonder you're able to give so many guys a start. I suppose you hire some of them right here on your ranch."

"That's the idea."

"It'll be fun to visit with them. I got to know some of them quite well when I flew them to Kelowna. I bet they're glad to be here instead of the jungles of Vietnam."

"You may not get a chance to see them," Kent said.

"Why not?"

"They don't eat with us. They have their own cook in the bunkhouse. Then they get up early to go to work in the fields."

"Oh. Well, maybe I can visit the bunkhouse after we eat."

"I don't see why not. But you might feel a little out of place. It's something like a men's locker room over there. The guys get pretty lax in the evenings. I don't mind. They deserve it after putting in a day's work."

"Is Millie your wife?" Debra, ever the journalist, asked.

The grin on Kent's face looked odd and out of place. "You could say that."

"I'd like to wash up before we eat," Blake said. "Would you show us where?"

"Sure, follow me. You, too, Debra." It sounded more like an order than an invitation. "I'll put you up in our guest room. It has a private bathroom attached."

"No need. We'll drive back to Kelowna after dinner," Blake said. "But thanks."

"Don't be silly," Kent said. "It's a long drive back to town, and it'll be dark. It'll be much more pleasant to drive in the morning when you can see the view."

"That makes sense," Debra agreed. "We may as well sleep here, don't you think, Blake?" Though Blake hadn't liked the contradiction, he understood Debra's desire. Apparently, Kent wasn't going to show them anything that night.

The guest room at the end of a long hallway was spacious and well furnished. "I'll leave you two to freshen up while I check on dinner," Kent said.

"Blake," Debra said when Kent was gone and the door closed. "I'm sorry. I didn't mean to contradict you. If you really don't want to spend the night here, I'm okay with that. We can leave right after dinner."

"No, you're right. You haven't had the chance to see your boys. Maybe we can get up early and go for a walk without Kent. It makes sense to wait until morning," Blake conceded with a sigh.

He didn't mention the really bad feeling he had about it, but shrugged it off as paranoia because of memories of Kent's childhood bullying. Instead he said, "I just can't believe this place is legitimate. Kent could not have changed that much. You notice he didn't tell us how he came into the kind of money this would take. Maybe he doesn't really own it."

"He doesn't seem to want me to talk to the boys." Debra says. "And I really want to."

"I know. And you should."

"Look at this room. I think it's Millie's," Debra said, holding open a closet door to reveal a full rack of dresses and blouses.

She opened a bureau drawer filled with neatly folded socks, panties, and bras. "See? They must not sleep together. Weird." In the bathroom, she found makeup and lotions that only a woman would use. "I hope she doesn't mind his giving us her room."

"Dinner's on the table." Kent opened the door without knocking, and Blake wondered how long he'd been standing outside the room.

They followed him to the dining room where Millie brought them platters of T-bone steak, baked potato, green beans, and a salad. She didn't sit, but hovered nearby to make sure they had everything they needed. It was delicious, and when finished, Debra thanked Millie and offered to help clean up.

Her offer was politely refused, so she asked for a tour of the greenhouses. Kent replied, "I'm afraid that will have to wait until morning. The lights don't work. It's on my list of things to fix. Hard to get to everything."

Kent led them to the den, a large room with too much furniture. The chair and sofa were wood framed with leather cushions that matched the décor of the house, but were too big to be comfortable. Coffee and end tables made of polished driftwood took up much of the space around the bearskin rug in the center of the floor. Kent turned on a couple of lamps and flopped into one of the big chairs. "Have a seat."

"It was all so good, I ate too much. I need to walk some of these calories off," Debra said. "If you'll excuse me, I'll get a bit of exercise while you guys catch up."

"You can't walk out there alone." Kent's voice rang with authority and disapproval. "You don't know the terrain, and there are mountain lions in these parts. It's really not safe. If you want to walk, I'll go with you."

So, they all headed down the long lane they'd driven in on. Kent insisted it had the easiest terrain to navigate in the receding light.

It was well after dark when they returned, and the bunkhouse was dark. Kent walked them all the way back to the room before wishing them good night.

"He's beginning to make me a claustrophobic," Debra whispered. "But I suppose he wants to take advantage of every minute with a brother he hasn't seen in years."

"Oh, I think it's you he wants to spend time with."

"Don't be silly. He's a married man."

"I wouldn't count on it."

"You don't seem to think much of him," Debra says.

"You wouldn't, either, if you knew him like I do."

"That hardly seems fair. People change."

"Maybe, but I'll be watching your back." Blake had noticed the way Kent ogled Debra, obvious lust in his eyes every time he looked at her.

Debra went into the bathroom with her overnight bag. When she came out, shaking her head, she said, "We were right about this being Millie's room. I see she's collected her makeup and toothbrush and things. I guess she'll be sleeping with her husband tonight."

They lay side by side, whispering until Debra fell

asleep. Blake stared into the dark, unable to shake the eerie feeling of being watched.

Blake pushed the memories aside and moaned as regrets flooded his mind. *Why didn't I insist we keep to our plan to stay in Kelowna instead of following him to his trap? Because I can never say no to Debra. Why didn't I go back and kill the bastard before he could kill her? Same reason, I guess.*

Debra, I'm sorry, so, so sorry. When you wanted to go to the cops, I convinced you it was a bad idea. We already knew the local police were protecting him. And even if we could get him charged with drug—or even human—trafficking, he'd get out on bond and come after you.

He closed his eyes, wishing he could block out what happened next—and their very narrow escape.

His brother had severely beaten him, breaking his arm and some ribs when he'd interrupted Kent's assault on Debra. As soon as his arm healed, Blake had gone to a pawn shop and spent a lot of money he couldn't afford for a Glock 19 pistol and lessons and practice at a shooting range to learn how to use it. He'd always been a pacifist and had never owned so much as a hunting rifle. But he knew of no way to protect Debra from the man intent on killing her, except to eliminate the monster.

But Debra had suspected his plan. She'd cried and begged him not to do it. "You'll either end up dead or in prison. Either way, I'd be without you, and I can't stand that."

He'd given in, and now he regretted it. But it might not be too late to save her life.

Kent had been vivid in his description of how he'd rape and pillage her for as long as he liked. "When I get tired of her, he'd promised, "You can be sure she'll never leave this place." And then the bastard had laughed. "But then who could ask for a prettier final resting place."

Blake didn't doubt Kent's word. His only hope of seeing Debra alive was to get there before Kent got tired of her. He swore again at Paul Diamond for not notifying him of her disappearance sooner. She'd been gone ten days before Garrigan contacted him.

True, Blake hadn't spoken to Debra since he walked out on her at Christmas time after learning the full extent of the secret she'd kept from him. She'd lied to him, when it came right down to it. And that just wasn't okay with him. *Migraine, my ass.* The enchantment or whatever the hell it was that took over her body that night and left her with no memory of it two days later was creepy.

Now Blake berated himself for not checking on her again, or going back to get rid of his brother even then. He'd thought he could forget her. *Ha! Forget the most beautiful, energetic, intelligent, and enigmatic woman he'd ever met? Fat chance.*

It was clear, now, with Debra gone, and her life in danger, there was no time to lose. He retrieved the gun from where he'd hidden it in the back of a tool box. He fueled his Cessna, stowed the Glock beside his seat, and flew north to the mountains of British Columbia.

CHAPTER 13

He intended to land somewhere north of Kent's ranch, hide the plane, and go in on foot, if he could find a place free of deep snow. A warm wind, known as a Chinook, had prevailed in the mountain valleys of southern British Columbia for some time, and Blake hoped that would make landing possible. In reality, there was no suitable clearing in the forested hills within a hundred miles of Kent's place. Flying back, he saw a perfect landing strip at the edge of an alfalfa field about a half mile north of Kent's house. There was only a fringe of snow next to the trees. He flew past it and cut his engine. He circled quietly, decreasing his air speed as he lost altitude until he was in line to touch down. He'd practiced this maneuver many times just so he'd know what to do if he ever lost an engine. He'd become proficient at judging his speed and elevation so he didn't come in too soon or too fast. He made a perfect landing, coasted to the end of the field, and braked to a full stop.

Jumping out, Glock in hand, Blake jogged toward the house and came to a huge field, probably the marijuana field Debra had described to him. Several men worked with shovels and trays of boxes across the field. He almost plowed into one before he saw him. The kid, who looked no more than eighteen, yelped and jumped up, blanching in fear.

"Sorry," Blake said. "I won't hurt you. I'm looking for Ken... I mean Sam Smith."

"Uh, why?" the young man asked, staring at the gun.

"I'm going to kill him," Blake replied, matter-of factly.

"Too late, man. He left a month ago."

"Where?"

The kid barked out a bitter laugh. "You think he'd tell us? All he said to us, besides telling us to work, was that we'd be shot on sight if we even thought of trying to leave. He left a couple of guards to make sure. I guarantee he wasn't kidding."

"So, two armed guards are holding all you guys prisoners?"

"One for the day shift and the other one all night. They sit down by the house and guard the road. There's only one way out of here without getting lost in the woods."

"You sure Smith isn't back yet?"

"Positive"

"What are you working on? It's a little early to plant, isn't it?"

Getting soil to test for pH factor. Sam's picky about having everything just right for his plants, so he left word to get it done if the snow melted enough. His guards make sure we always have something to do."

"What's that?" Blake jerked his head up as he heard the roar of a motorcycle approaching through the trees.

"Gotta go. I can't let him catch me not working. I'd run, if I was you," the kid said. "Unless you're looking for a gun fight."

Blake wasn't—not with a stranger. He ran for the trees at the edge of the field. He came to kill one man, and one man only. If he was going to prison it would be in exchange for Kent's death and Debra's freedom.

As he slipped deeper into the forest, bullets strafed the trees and zinged over his head to the rat-a-tat tune of machine gun fire. He dropped to the ground and lay flat until the shooting stopped. Then he scurried on all fours farther into the woods, raised to a low crouch, and angled northeast with a plan to circle back to the Cessna.

He heard the motorcycle rev up and head in the direction of the airplane.

Damn. He'll get there before I can.

Apparently, the man had no desire to chase Blake through the trees, and he didn't need to.

When Blake thought he'd gone far enough to parallel the landing strip, he edged closer until he could see through the trees. He lay on his stomach on the soft duff among the ferns where he had a narrow view between foliage to watch the watcher. The ground was damp, though little snow remained. The man sitting on the motorcycle was huge. Dressed in camo fatigues, the man straddled the bike, his massive arms crossed over his broad chest. An assault rifle rested across the handlebars. He faced the edge of the trees where Blake lay, both men waiting.

Blake didn't move, but his mind wouldn't stop. The earthy pine-scented smell of the forest, the crisp air, and the proximity to the house stirred his memory into a vivid replay of the morning after eating at Kent's table and sleeping in Millie's bedroom.

He remembered waking to find Debra gone. He'd pulled on his jeans and shoes in a near panic. He knew she wanted to go for a walk before Kent got up, but he was supposed to go with her. Outside, in the pre-dawn light, he looked for her in every direction and then started up the path that led in the opposite direction from the driveway. As he jogged up the narrow, well-worn trail, he was glad for the lack of gravel making his footsteps nearly soundless. He hadn't gone far before he heard voices. *Debra!*

"Stop. I said no. I will never make love to you."

Blake sped faster, as he heard his brother's maniacal laugh. "Did you hear me ask you? What makes you think you have a choice?"

Blake grabbed a dead tree limb that hung down from a fir tree at the edge of the path. It broke off easily in his hand. He ran past the small opening in the trees, as he scanned the trail ahead.

"Nooo!" Debra screamed, until the scream turned to a gurgle and stopped.

Blake skidded to a halt, stepped back and saw his brother crouched over Debra's prone form, his palm pressing on her throat, his other hand tearing at Debra's jeans.

Blake lunged at his brother, swinging hard and catching the right side of Kent's face with enough force to lift him off of Debra. Kent landed in a heap—next to the broken end of the tree branch that had snapped on contact. Debra rolled to her knees, gasping.

"Deb!" Blake yelled. "Run! If you can get up, run as fast as you can."

He watched her scramble to her feet, hit the trail running, and disappear from his sight, just as a blow to his head knocked him to the ground and filled his vision with stars. When he could see straight, Kent loomed over him, swinging the club at his head. Blake dodged and dived at Kent's feet. Too late. The blow caught him on the shoulder. He thought he felt something snap. Before he could roll away, Kent's steel-toed boots slammed into his rib cage.

Blake curled into a fetal position, and moaned, "Stop."

Kent didn't stop. The tree-limb club came down on his ribs as a boot stomped his wrist. Blake had never felt such pain.

"Get up," Kent ordered.

Blake raised his head to stare into the bore of a very big handgun.

"Get the hell up," Kent said.

It wasn't easy with one arm hanging useless and his every breath knifing his chest cavity, but he struggled to his feet.

"I'm going to teach you not to meddle in my activities, little brother. I could kill you right now, but I don't think you've suffered enough. You need some mental agony, too."

"You were about to kill my girlfriend, you bastard."

"My girlfriend now, bro. She is way too classy for the likes of you. Get used to it. She's mine, and guess what. You're going to watch me have my way with her. I'm going to have her every which way I want, ways your naive, little pea brain never imagined. And the more she fights, the better it is for me."

"Damn you!"

"No, you be damned. You're gonna watch while I rape and mutilate her. You'll hear her beg for mercy, but you won't be able to lift a finger to help her. Oh, yeah. She's going to see which of the Mallory brothers is the real man. Pretty soon she'll find she likes it. And then I'll let her kill you."

With the barrel of his pistol poking into Blake's spine,

Kent pushed his brother to the house and into a back door. He frisked him, took his car keys, and shoved him into the bedroom. As Blake landed on the floor, he heard the lock click. He didn't try to move.

Debra, oh baby, I'm so sorry! I never learned to fight, and I'm obviously no good at it. What kind of man am I?

Blake made it to the bed just before the door opened and Debra was shoved in. The door slammed shut and locked. His vision was so blurred in the eye that wasn't swollen closed, that he couldn't see her face clearly. But her voice told him how horrified she was at his appearance.

She gasped as the door slammed behind her. "Oh, Blake. Oh, God, what has he done to you? I'm so sorry." She touched him, and he winced. She covered her mouth and stared.

He could barely see her, but he was sure those were tears streaming down her face.

"How could I run when you were fighting to save me? I panicked. I didn't know what I was doing." She sobbed. "I'll never forgive myself."

He tried to tell her it was okay, that it was what he wanted her to do, but his mouth wasn't working right.

"Where do you hurt the most?"

"My arm. I think it's broken. Ribs, too," he slurred, sounding like he had a mouthful of mud. "You hurt?"

"No, thanks to you." Debra reached for him, but he yelped, "Don't," and she jumped back.

She knelt beside the bed, and with his good hand, he touched her face, wiping tears away.

"You need a doctor. We've got to get out of here."

He put a finger to his lips. "Paper? Pen?" he mouthed.

"Bugged?" Debra whispered.

He nodded and said, loud enough for Kent to hear if he was listening, "Kent took the car keys. I don't think I'll be seeing a doctor."

"I know. He showed me. The bastard," Debra said, following his lead like he knew she would. She patted her pocket to assure him she still had the extra key. "What can I do to make it stop hurting so much?"

"You got any aspirin?"

"I'm looking. I might have something in my purse. If not, I'll go ask Kent for something."

"No," he moaned. "Don't leave me."

With her tears fresh in his memory, he felt the all-too-familiar sting in his eyes. He closed them and thought, *Damn it, Deb. I've failed you again. Where the hell does Kent have you. God, I hope I find you alive. But first I have to get out of here without getting killed.*

The guard exhibited extreme patience. Straddling the Harley, his arms crossed, and the rifle propped in front of him, he sat still as a statue staring at the trees where Blake lay.

CHAPTER 14

When Garrigan asked the three men to meet with him again, Josh refused to come to San Francisco. "I'll meet you in my office at Randall Aircraft. Paul and Blake can come to LA easier than I can get away to go sit in my daughter's empty apartment again. I don't see the point."

Garrigan complied with Randall's wishes, not because of any urge to kowtow to the man, but because he hoped he'd learn something fresh at the place Debra had worked alongside her father. Maybe he'd get a better sense of their relationship. Paul agreed to meet him there. Garrigan left messages but didn't hear from Blake. *Maybe he'll just show up,* Garrigan thought. He wasn't counting on it, though.

A young and attractive receptionist ushered him into a plush office. Paul was already there, seated in one of the upholstered armchairs in front of a large, gleaming mahogany desk. "Mr. Randall will be with you shortly," the young woman said. "May I get you something to drink?"

"Water, please," Garrigan said.

When she'd gone from the room, he nodded to Paul and thanked him for the newspaper articles he'd brought over. "May I ask you some questions while we wait for Mr. Randall?"

"Sure," Paul said, looking wary, as if afraid of what emotions more questions might evoke.

"The day we were all together in Debra's apartment, we were discussing jewelry. I got the impression that you may have thought of something that Josh had over-looked. Am I right?"

Paul seemed to relax a little, but he took time to choose his words. "Debra had a favorite pendant that she wore more than any other jewelry," he said. "It was a piece of pyramid shaped cut glass on a gold chain—a prism. I don't think it's in her apartment, but that probably just means that she was wearing it when she left."

Garrigan made note of that in his book, though he didn't see how it would help. "Was there any particular significance to this prism?"

Paul shrugged. "No, other than she seemed to like it a lot. It wasn't all that pretty, kind of big, and definitely not expensive like most of the jewelry her father gave her over the years."

"Who gave her the prism?"

"Her dad."

Garrigan made another notation, but seeing nothing in this information that shed any light on her disappear-ance, he moved on with his questions.

"Did you think of anything else that might help since we met last?"

Paul hesitated for only a moment. "Nothing. Have you found any more leads?" Paul still wasn't telling him everything. Garrigan was sure of it.

Garrigan shook his head. "I thought of a couple more things I'd like to ask Mallory, but I couldn't reach him. Do you know anything about his whereabouts?"

Garrigan watched an expression of contempt cloud Paul's face. "No. We don't exactly keep in touch. He and Debra broke up for a while. I thought it was for good."

This surprised Garrigan, and he wondered if that was

why Mallory was not answering his calls. "What caused the breakup, do you know?"

Paul looked down and shrugged. "Just incompatibility, I guess. They didn't have all that much in common—other than they both like to fly. And then she saw him with another woman. She was upset about that, but I told her it was good riddance. If a guy can't appreciate Debra as she is, then she shouldn't waste her time with him."

"And what was it about her that he couldn't accept?"

Paul shrugged. "Nobody's perfect, but Debra comes damned close."

Not an answer, Garrigan thought, and wondered why, but, for now, he let it go as he made another notation.

"Was Debra writing or had she written a book that you know of?"

"No. I'm sure I'd know if she were. Why do you ask?"

"It's what I wanted to talk to Mallory about. There was a manuscript in one of her desk drawers. When I went back to her apartment, it wasn't there anymore. I suspect that Blake took it, and I wonder why."

"What manuscript? I mean, did it have a title—and author? Maybe she was editing it for someone."

"I didn't get a good look at it, nor did I find any detail about it in the inventory by investigators who went through her office." Garrigan watched Paul closely as he added, "The title was *Canadian Odyssey*, I believe."

Paul just looked puzzled. "Never heard of it."

The door flew open, and Josh Randall breezed into the room with an imperious air. "Sorry if I kept you waiting. There was a problem on the assembly line that had to be dealt with before production could proceed."

He enthroned himself behind the big desk and leaned forward, bestowing a practiced smile on Garrigan. "If we could get on with this meeting, I, for one, have pressing business to attend to."

"More pressing than finding your daughter?" Garrigan asked in a thinly controlled voice.

The smile disappeared quickly from Randall's face. "Of course not, but unless you have something new, I don't know what you expect to accomplish with this meeting. Do you?"

"Mostly more questions, some that I hope you will answer."

"I don't know any more than I did the last time I saw you."

"There was a picture on her bookshelf that isn't there anymore. What can you tell me about that, Josh?"

Randall's face darkened, and his jaw clenched, but the countenance changed so quickly to one of nonchalance that Garrigan had to wonder if he imagined it. "What's to tell? It's a school picture of Debra's mother."

"And you took it. Why?"

"Because I don't have one like it, and I want to make a photocopy. I plan to give it back to her, if you ever find her."

There was no mistaking the contempt in Josh Randall's voice. Garrigan, sure the man was not leveling with him, wondered why.

"Tell me about her mother."

"What about her?"

"Everything. I only know that she is no longer living. How did she die?"

"Accidental drowning." Josh growled. "So what? Debra wasn't even two years old when it happened. She doesn't even remember her mother."

"Yet she had this picture on her bookcase."

"So?"

"You seemed surprised by it. Is it something she has recently acquired?"

"How would I know, and what damned difference does it make? If this is your only question, I'm going back to work. I have much more important things to do than discuss things that are completely irrelevant to the case."

"I'll decide what's relevant," Garrigan growled back. He glanced at his notes and back at the two men. "Can either of you tell me why she was renting a car—actually various cars, or why she spent a few months in a string of cheap motels while she continued to pay the rent on her apartment?"

The look of surprise and disbelief on both men's faces told him more than their words.

"What the hell are you talking about? Why would she do that? I don't believe it," Randall roared.

"You must be mistaken," Paul said. "I'm sure she'd tell me if she wasn't staying at her apartment."

"I found a brochure from the Lazy J Motel in her mail with an evaluation form and a letter saying, 'We hope you'll come again.' I spoke with the manager. It was Debra Randall's signature—though not her name—on the rental agreement. The description he gave me verified it was Debra who stayed in the apartment."

"Are you suggesting she was having an affair with some slime ball?" Randall roared.

"Not at all. She was never seen with another person. No one else ever came to the studio apartment she rented. Further investigation shows that she'd stayed in other motels before the Lazy J. She used an alias, a different one each time, but we've verified that it was her signature and her description."

"What does this mean?" Paul asked.

"My guess is that she was hiding from someone. She must have feared for her life to go to such lengths. I was hoping you could tell me what she was afraid of."

Paul was quiet for some time, apparently thinking. Garrigan watched him and waited.

"Like I said, she was getting mail at the paper," Paul said. "Then I told her about a phone call from someone wanting to know her address. She didn't seem to take it too seriously at first, but for just a moment, when I told her the guy's name, she looked—I don't know—alarmed, I guess."

"What was his name?"

"Sam Smith. But she agreed it was probably a made-up name. She was still a little paranoid, so I put extra locks on her door. That seemed to satisfy her."

"Apparently it didn't, but it seems she didn't want you to know that."

Paul appeared to be hurt by this pronouncement. He didn't respond.

"Just one more question, Mr. Randall, before we adjourn. What do you know about the manuscript for a book called *Canadian Odyssey*?"

"I have no idea what you're talking about."

"It was in her desk drawer, and then it wasn't. I believe Blake Mallory may have it. Do you have any idea where I might find him?"

"No. We don't keep in touch." Grim-faced, Josh Randall seemed to struggle with what to say next. Garrigan waited.

"I hope you find him soon. I doubt he's telling us all he knows."

Garrigan doubted that any of them were.

CHAPTER 15

Blake patched holes in the right wing and fuselage of his Cessna. He'd arrived back in Marfa exhausted, but unable to sleep. So, he worked on his plane.

He'd fallen asleep there in the soft ground amid the undergrowth as he waited for a chance to get to his plane. He hadn't meant to, wary that the guard would give up, get off his bike, and come looking for him. Blake awakened in darkness to the roar of the motorcycle. He watched the guard leave the field and disappear in the trees in the direction of the house.

Blake crawled out of the forest into moonlight and sprinted to his plane. To his great relief, it started. He hadn't expected it to, figuring the guard would have disabled it. He'd just turned the plane around to head up the runway, when a motorcycle appeared alongside him driven by a smaller, older man, probably the night guard. Blake powered up the runway as fast as the plane would go, but the guard on the bike had no trouble keeping pace with him. A shot rang out and Blake looked into the face of the grinning guard. He wielded a sub machine gun with his left hand while steering with his right.

Blake could only thank the rough terrain the motorcycle bounced over that he wasn't hit. He'd managed to pull the plane up at the end of the runway, just clearing the trees as more shots hit the underbelly of his aircraft.

By the time he finished patching holes, exhaustion won out and he crashed on the worn couch in his office. Two hours later, he woke up, made a fresh pot of coffee, and picked up the manuscript.

Now he'd see Debra's account of Kent's assault.

I woke early. I slept well in the curl of Blake's arm and warm body. He was still asleep, so I slipped out of bed as quietly as I could. As I tiptoed down the hall into the living room, I heard the soft breathing of someone asleep on the couch. Millie! How strange. I went out the front door, opening and closing it as noiselessly as possible.

What a glorious day. The sun was just coming up over the mountain. I love to be up and outdoors before anyone else, especially here. Kent was giving me the creeps. I checked out the greenhouses and found padlocks on the doors. The double layers of Visqueen were too steamed up on the inside for me to identify the plants growing inside.

I followed a narrow but well-worn path toward a small building. Locked! I walked on, following the path as it continued through the woods. I'd gone about a hundred yards when Kent stepped out in front of me. I stifled a scream when I saw who it was.

"Looking for something?" he asked.

I laughed, embarrassed. "Kent! You scared me. I didn't think anyone else was awake."

"Obviously. Well, I'm not a sound sleeper. What are you looking for?"

"Nothing. I'm just out for my customary morning walk. I thought it would be nice to see your beautiful place while getting my daily exercise."

"I'll go with you and show you around."

I said, "Okay," hoping I didn't sound as disappointed as I felt.

I followed him a little farther up the path until he stopped and turned so abruptly that I smacked into him. He grabbed me, pinning my arms to my side.

"I've been wanting to make love to you since the first time I saw you. Thanks for giving me this chance."

"Stop. Let me go. I'm not making love to you."

"I'm not asking," he growled.

He pushed me off the path into a small clearing and, wrapping his leg behind my ankles, knocked me to the ground. Dropping on top of me, he clamped his foul-tasting mouth on mine, held me down with one hand around my throat, and unzipped my jeans with the other. I jerked my head to the side and screamed. He tightened his grip on my throat, and my screams turned into a croak until my breath was completely cut off. I bucked and clawed at his hands trying to pull them off, but he only pressed harder on my throat.

Just when I thought I would die, he lifted off of me. I was suddenly free. I rolled onto my knees and scrambled to my feet. Blake stood in a sumo-wrestler position with the stub of a tree branch in both hands. Kent lay sprawled on the ground with blood gushing from a cut on the side of his head next to his eye.

Blake yelled, "Run!"

I ran.

Terrified, I sped up the path farther into the woods, running blindly. I skidded to a stop when I came to an open field.

It took me a moment to realize what I was looking at—a forest of marijuana, acres of it in various stages of growth, some of it twice as tall as I am.

"Vegetables, my eye," I muttered.

I heard a rustling sound behind me and started running again. I veered to my left along the edge of the field and dove back into the forest, too winded to run any farther. I crawled through thick undergrowth beneath towering evergreen trees. When I thought I was hidden, I lay still and tried to control my raspy breath.

"Debra?" Was that Blake or Kent's voice? I wasn't sure. I held my breath and he called again. Kent. My heart nearly stopped, sure that if Kent was alive, Blake was dead.

"Well, you've got to come out sometime, sweet thing. There's no way out of here except by the road. Just ask the boys." Kent's laugh sent chills up my spine. I didn't move.

I don't know how long I lay there, frozen in fear and grief. When fear turned to shame for my cowardice, I crawled to the edge of the field and peered out. A man stood not three feet from me, cutting down plants and laying them on a cart. When I recognized him, I stood up.

"Hi, Jake."

He jumped at the sound of my voice.

"Miss Randall. What are you doing here?"

His voice was filled with terror, the fear he'd shown me on the plane multiplied ten times.

"Jake, are you all right? I had no idea this was the kind of operation I was getting you involved in."

Jacob looked over his shoulder and quickly back at me. "If Sam finds out you're here, he'll kill you."

"Are you in danger?"

"I will be if he catches me talking to you."

Jake was thinner than when I first met him, if possible, but his acne was gone, revealing a handsome, but still boyish face. My presence was making him nervous, but I needed to know more.

"I'll slip back into the trees, then, so he can't see me if he comes. If you see him, just start whistling or something, and don't look at me. I'll make myself scarce."

"Okay." His voice quavered.

I ducked into the trees and slid under a leafy bush. "Does he treat you okay? Are you here because you want to be?"

"We're all stuck here." Jacob looked furtively at the path that led to the house. "Joe tried walking out, but Sam's like a cat. He's up all night I think, watching the road. I think he's got the bunkhouse bugged."

"Then you guys are prisoners."

"Slaves, I'd call it. We work sun up to sundown in the fields or the labs or the green houses."

"Does he pay you?"

"Room and board and a few bucks to send

home once a month to keep our families from worrying about us. We write letters, but I'm pretty sure he reads them to make sure we don't say anything that would make them think everything isn't just hunky dory."

"This is terrible. I'm sure Ellen had no idea this was going on. She thinks Kent is getting you jobs and finding you places to live."

"Who's Kent?"

"Oh, I mean Sam."

"Why'd you call him Kent?"

"Never mind. It doesn't matter. But the guy has to be exposed and shut down."

"Be careful. He kills people who cross him. Joe..." Jacob coughed, pushed the cart farther up the row, and cut down the next plant.

I wiggled farther back into the foliage, as Kent sauntered over to Jacob.

"Kind of slow this morning, aren't you? That cart ought to be full by now," Kent growled. "What've you been doing?"

"Just feeling a little off, today, boss," Jacob said, "I think I'm coming down with some-thing."

"No excuses. Speed it up—while I dig out this babe you been shooting the breeze with. That is all you were doing, right? Shooting the breeze?"

Jacob didn't answer, but his red face, break-ing out in perspiration, spoke volumes.

Suddenly, I found myself staring into Kent's pale brown eyes where I had seen his boots a moment before. The eye beside the bloody gash was swollen closed. "Come on out, darlin'.

I think your big, brave boyfriend is worried about you."

He grabbed my wrist and dragged me out on my belly. "I'll settle with you later, Jake. Now get to work."

Twisting my arm behind my back, Kent pushed me ahead of him toward the house.

"What have you done to Blake? Where is he?" I yelled.

"You're worried now? You sure didn't stay around to defend him when he came to your rescue, did you? I should kill you both, but I've decided to wait till morning. You know why?"

I didn't answer.

"Two reasons. One, I don't want Millie to get suspicious. And two, I intend to finish what I started this morning before my brother so rudely interrupted. And not just once, but over and over again, and with an audience. Oh, that makes it so much sweeter. And little bro? How fun to see him squirm and unable to get to you. It'll go easier for you if you don't resist." He paused and laughed. "But fight all you want. It'll just make it all more exciting for me."

"Never, you bastard," I growled.

He jerked my arm up so hard I yelped.

"And my brother?" Kent continued as if he hadn't nearly pulled my arm from its socket. "If he's lucky, I'll let him watch your torture for days. But if he causes a problem, I'll just have to eliminate him. I'll keep you until I get bored of you. But you won't ever leave. Not alive."

Clamping my mouth closed, I did everything in my power to keep from screaming out in pain.

"I'm sending Millie to visit her sister in the states. When the whole house is ours, the fun will begin."

I stumbled. He jerked me to my feet, wrenching my arm harder.

He opened the door to Millie's bedroom, but before shoving me through it, he dangled the rental car keys in front of my face. "Don't even think about leaving, not that Blakey boy's in any shape to drive."

CHAPTER 16

Blake put the journal pages down and rubbed his eyes. The memory of that night would stay with him forever. The only thing that had saved them was Debra's independence. She'd insisted on having her own key to the rental car. Kent hadn't suspected that. He planned, with Deb's help, to break a window and escape as soon as Kent left to take Millie to Kelowna to put her on a plane. Those hopes were dashed when Kent strode into the room.

He said, "I wouldn't want you to go hungry while I'm gone, so I brought you some lunch," Kent said. He carried a muffin and a glass of purple liquid. "I couldn't leave without getting you something to eat, Babe."

"I'm not hungry," Debra said, backing away.

"You'll eat. I'm not leaving this room until you've eaten every bite and downed every drop." He set the tray on the bureau and twisted her arm behind her back. He picked up the muffin. The more she resisted, the harder he wrenched her arm.

Blake tried to get up, but fell back in excruciating pain.

"Don't even think of interfering, bro," Kent jeered. "You'll just make it harder on her."

Tears ran down her cheeks as she swallowed the pungent liquid he poured in her mouth. He didn't stop force-feeding her until the muffin and drink were gone. He picked up a suitcase, then, and filled it with clothing from Millie's closet and drawers. "I'll be back later tonight," he said, "but I imagine you'll be asleep." He left the room, laughing. The door closed with an ominous click.

Debra jiggled the doorknob. Locked. Unlike most bedroom doors, there was no way to unlock it from the inside. "We're locked in."

"Come lie down before you pass out. Whatever he gave you will act fast," Blake warned.

"Wait." Debra rummaged through her purse, dug out a bottle of Excedrin, filled a glass of water, and staggered to the bed. "Take this for your pain. It's all I have." By the time she reached the bed, she was wobbling.

"Lie down!" Blake had yelped, taking the water from her.

She climbed—more like fell—over him and crumpled, spilling half the water. The bottle rolled to the floor. Blake downed what was left of the water but didn't attempt to retrieve the bottle. Even if he could reach it, he wouldn't be able to open it. He couldn't even wiggle the fingers of his right hand. Blake tried to awaken Debra who lay against him, leaving him little room to breathe. She didn't budge.

The pain was so bad, Blake thought he would pass out and wished to high heaven he would. After a few hours that seemed like an eternity, he heard Kent's vehicle approaching. In minutes, Kent stalked into the room and shook Debra. She didn't respond.

"Oh, well, I didn't expect her to be awake yet. I'll be back."

"Kent, how about something for pain?" Blake begged.

Kent opened the door. "Nah. You need to stay awake and think about what a bad idea it is to interrupt your big bro in the middle of his love making."

"You son of a bitch. You call that love making?"

"I was set to enjoy it. But don't worry. I'll get plenty of chances. And as long as I don't get tired of you, I'll let you watch." He laughed as he went out, locking the door behind him.

He came again in the morning and shook Debra, who showed no sign of waking.

"Like I said," Kent boasted. "I'm a patient man. We've got all the time I'll ever need. She'll wake up eventually, and then the fun will begin."

He didn't come back until after dark. When he still couldn't rouse Debra, he cursed. "What the hell? I didn't intend to give her enough to sleep forever. She must really be a lightweight."

"She doesn't drink, and I doubt she's ever taken anything stronger than aspirin."

"Shit! Oh well. Tomorrow." He started toward the door, but turned around with a leer twisting his half-drunken face. "Do you enjoy porn, little brother? You'll soon get to. Your little girlfriend will be the star." He leaned close, his beer breath strong in Blake's face, and slurred, "I'll show you some BDSM like you've never imagined it. That should get your mind off your pain." He staggered out of the room but didn't forget to lock the door behind him.

Blake didn't know how much time had lapsed when he felt Debra stir beside me. He put his hand over her mouth until she opened her eyes. Pointing to the overhead light fixture, he whispered, "The bug."

Debra nodded and lay perfectly still for a moment before gingerly testing each limb. Getting up as quietly as possible, she stood on the bed, and, by the pale moon-light and by feel, pulled down the small microphone from the side of the ceiling light. She removed the battery.

"Good," Blake whispered. "We don't dare turn on the light or he might see it under the door or through the window. There's a penlight in my back pack." He slid off the bed and stood. Supporting his arm and fighting the urge to cry out in pain, he went to the bathroom and re-trieved the belt to the terrycloth robe that hung on the back of the door. With his mouth next to Debra's ear, he whispered, "He might have heard something, so we have to hurry. Tie this around me to keep my arm against my chest."

She did.

"Now my jacket. Put it over my shoulders and tie the sleeves together—tighter."

When his arm was as immobile as possible, he told her, "Now. Break the window and push out the screen. Crawl out and run. Get the car started and wait for me unless you see him coming. If you do, drive away as fast as you can. Don't worry about me."

Debra tried the window. It was locked and the fas-tener welded down. Was Millie a prisoner, too? Debra tapped the window, then hit it with all her strength with the tapered end the small flashlight. Blake winced at the sound of breaking glass. The noise could not be helped. They cleared away the remaining edges as quickly and quietly as possible. Debra went through the window first and turned to help Blake. They ran together. Debra sup-porting him as they crept through the dim light from a quarter moon.

"Go," Blake said. "I'll catch up."

"No way. I deserted you once. I won't again."

Once in the car, Debra drove slowly and carefully, knowing that every bump caused Blake pain.

"I'm glad you insisted on having your own key. It pays to have an independent girlfriend."

"See?" She smiled, then added more soberly. "I never thought I'd need it like this. What a nightmare!"

"Do you feel any effects from the drugs he gave you?"

"No. I'm surprisingly alert, but I guess that's the adrenalin. Whatever he gave me wasn't very strong, for me to be this wide awake this soon."

"Soon? You slept the rest of Sunday, Sunday night, and through Monday. It's Tuesday morning."

"Really?"

"Yeah. Kent was furious yesterday when he couldn't rouse you."

The clock on the dash said 2:47. Blake hoped Kent would sleep several more hours. That hope was dashed in a minute.

"What was that?"

"What?" Debra asked.

"I saw a flash of light. Listen." Blake paused only a moment. "Gun it, Debra. Kent's following us. Don't worry about the bumps. If I pass out, just keep going. Don't let him catch us."

They bounced over rocks and brushed through overhanging tree branches, but Debra didn't slow down. Kent had the advantage of knowing the terrain, and he was driving a jeep.

They came upon the gravel road suddenly, going too fast. Debra stomped the brake once, but then tromped on the accelerator as she cranked the wheel to the right.

The car skidded around the corner and fishtailed, but she straightened it out and sped down the narrow road.

"Damn. You must have been a race-car driver in another life."

Headlights appeared behind them.

"I wish I knew this road better," Debra said, "If I remember right, there are some hairpin turns."

Blake didn't comment, but vividly imagined them launching off the road into a deep ravine. But they didn't. Debra slowed enough to maneuver through corners without losing control in the gravel. Kent gained on them. By the time they came to the paved highway, he was right on their tail.

On the pavement, Debra gunned it and gradually outdistanced him. Approaching a small town, little more than a wide spot in the road, she barely let off the gas. Flashing lights came on behind them.

"Shoot. I'm going to have to stop. But I can tell him…"

"If you tell him about Kent, he won't believe you."

"But maybe the cop will detain him for…" Debra began as she pulled over.

"Please, Debra. We don't want to be the ones detained."

Debra nodded and rolled down the window.

"You seem to be in an awful hurry, miss."

"Uh, yes. I was. I am. My boyfriend's badly hurt, and I'm trying to get him to the hospital."

The officer looked at Blake.

"What happened?" he asked.

"I was trying out a friend's motorcycle. Ran off the road and hit a tree."

"Take my advice and stay off those things," the officer said. Straightening, he added. "And you, miss. Slow down. You want to get him there alive, don't you? You'll have to go all the way to Kelowna to find a hospital."

"Thank you," Debra breathed and put the car in gear.

Headlights bloomed in the rear-view mirrors as the Jeep swept over the hill. The lights blinked off and back on three times in quick succession. Was it some kind of warning?

"Wait," the officer said, reaching through the window to grasp her arm. "I'm going to have to write you a ticket for speeding. Give me your driver's license and registration."

Debra began shuffling through her purse as Blake opened the glove box—and yelped in pain.

The officer didn't wait. "I'll be right back. Don't go anywhere."

"But..." Debra began. But the man was gone, striding back past his cruiser, to the approaching jeep.

"Punch it, Deb. Get out of here as fast as you can."

Punch it, she did. "Kent wasn't warning us," she said, "He was signaling the cop."

"Yep. Kent jumped in the cruiser with him."

The patrol car started up, lights still flashing and the siren blaring.

"I could outrun a Jeep, but the cruiser's gaining on me," Deb moaned.

"Don't give up. If they stop us, with the police backing Kent, we don't have a chance. If we can just get to Kelowna, we might get help."

Debra pushed the rental car to its top speed, and still the cruiser kept up. When it pulled out to pass, Debra managed to keep ahead, not letting him get in front of them. They were side by side when they rounded a corner and saw a semi bearing down on them. She jerked the car onto the shoulder, missing the truck by inches.

They heard squealing tires and the crash of metal on metal. In the side mirror, Blake saw the truck weave, rock, and land on its side with the trailer crosswise in the road and the cab in the ditch. He couldn't see the cruiser.

Blake told her to go to the airport instead of the hospital. "We can't trust anyone this close to Kent. Let's get to the states."

Debra drove through an open gate, parked the rental car next to the Raptor, and jumped out, leaving the keys in the ignition. She helped Blake climb into the Raptor.

Blake shook the memory from his head and refilled his coffee cup. Time to come up with a new plan. He needed to get more forceful or at least more specific in order to learn Kent's whereabouts from his mother.

CHAPTER 17

The feelings welling in his mid-section were so reminiscent of his childhood, that Blake wanted to turn back. He'd spent years recovering from the worst trauma in his life, and now he was winging toward the source of his greatest heartbreak.

Blake had grown up in a small town in Colorado, the son of the town drunk. It was a town where names categorized you. And in that town, "Mallory" meant worthless. It hadn't been so bad in the early years when Mom was still home.

Mom. His vision of Ellen Mallory, before she left and changed her name, was vivid and painful. She had been his life, his anchor in the midst of constant anxiety, the only spot of hope to hold onto. And then she was gone.

She was an independent sort who swore it didn't matter what people said—it only mattered what you did and what you were. Tall, slender, with dark hair and deep blue eyes like his own, she'd married Jack Mallory when she was sixteen and he was stationed in Texas at an Air Force base near San Antonio. Blake had no idea what she had seen in him. He was handsome, but anyone could see he was weak. Blake's older brother, Kent, had been born a year later, and the small family returned to Jack's Colorado home.

Jack went to work at the local airport but was soon fired because of the boozing. Ellen Mallory, now pregnant with Blake, got a job cooking in the local café to support them. Typically, the town tolerated the good-natured, drunken Jack Mallory, but the people there hated Ellen with her "snooty airs." She apparently tried to ignore them and managed to hold her little family together by hiding her paychecks from her sodden husband. Jack stayed sober only long enough to earn beer money for the next binge.

Ellen poured all the love in her affectionate nature into her sons. When they were little, they were so protected by their mother's devotion they didn't know what the rest of the town thought of them. When they found out, they reacted in different ways.

Kent Mallory was endowed with his father's natural charm and ease with people. He soon learned that people like to be right. Folks expected him to be wild and irresponsible—after all, he was a Mallory. When Kent started drinking when he was fourteen, he began treating his mother with the same scorn the rest of the town did. It was subtle at first, then openly abusive. Jack, who worshiped Ellen in his lucid moments, was by now almost constantly in an alcoholic stupor and didn't notice his son's behavior. Blake, who had always adored his brother, was dumbfounded.

Blake was thirteen years old and had long since learned that the world consisted of a father who was either gone or lying in bed in various states of intoxication, a mother who was the sunshine of his existence but usually working, and an irrepressible, domineering older brother, who often led them into one scrape or another. He also had school, with all those books that told of wonderful things and places, and the town's small airport where he washed airplanes for 25 cents each.

One night, when Blake came home from his job at the airport, he was astonished to hear shouting from the kitchen.

"Kent Mallory. How could you?" His mother's voice quavered with tears and anger.

"Nothin' to it, Ma. I just tipped up the bottle and down she went." Kent's voice was slurred but impertinent.

Blake stopped, stunned.

"Oh, Kent. You've seen what booze did to your father—to us. For God's sake, you're only a child." She was sobbing now.

The sound mobilized him. He had never heard his mother cry.

She was standing at the kitchen sink, her work-reddened hands covering her face, her shoulders shaking. Blake stared.

"Oh, come off it," Kent drawled. "Who do you think you are to be talking so high and mighty? You're just a damned cook. Quit going around thinking you're better than everybody else. Nobody likes you—nobody."

Blake looked at his brother, horrified. His mother made a small choking sound and left the kitchen. He followed her to the bedroom where she sat on the edge of the bed, tears streaming down her white face.

Still she sat there, motionless but for the tears that fell silently. Blake approached her tentatively and touched her hand, searching her face, looking for his warm, loving mother in the eyes of this stranger. She looked at his hand but made no move to grasp it. She sat there a long time and with each minute, Blake's fear grew larger, almost smothering him. When she finally raised her head, he noticed that the usual sparkle had disappeared from her eyes.

"He told a lie, Mom. Everybody likes you. I like you. I love you."

Her lips trembled, and she finally took his hand.

"Listen very carefully, Blake. You must learn to rely on yourself. There isn't anyone else in the world you can count on. Do you understand me? There's only you, Blake—only you to make sure your dreams come true. Only you to blame if they don't. Will you remember that?"

Her words didn't help his fear. He didn't understand.

"Blake?"

"Yes, I'll remember."

"Good. Now, I'm going to bed. See if you can find yourself some supper, okay?"

"Okay."

Blake left her room, shaken by her tears, worried about the words he didn't comprehend, and certain that a light had gone out of his world.

Kent was sprawled in a kitchen chair, smiling stupidly at the empty gin bottle in his fist. Kent, though only a year older than Blake, stood at least six inches taller. Nonetheless, Blake walked over and looked down at his brother, and the fear that had gripped him turned to anger. "If you ever talk to her like that again, I'll kill you."

Kent was far too drunk to take notice of the warning. He looked at Blake vacantly and slumped to the floor.

Blake never saw or heard from his mother again until all those years later in Los Angeles with Debra. No note, not a single letter. He didn't even know if she was alive, though his dad said, "She's fine. Gone off in a huff. She'll be back when she finds out she can't live without us."

But she didn't come back.

Blake moped around for days, but finally, taking his mother's last words of advice, determined to make a life for himself. He spent most of his time at the small airport when he wasn't in school. Sometimes he didn't even go home to sleep at the small shack his father had moved them into when he no longer had his wife's salary for rent.

Blake saved all the wages he earned at the airport. The owner gave him more work, teaching him to take an engine apart, find the problem, fix it, and put it back together. Blake's expertise had grown, and his boss taught him to fly. By the time he graduated high school, he started looking for a place of his own. When he heard of a small, dying airport in Marfa, Texas, he had just enough money saved for the down payment.

The surprise of finding his mother alive in the little dive in LA brought back such pain, he'd avoided meeting her again—which wasn't hard, as she hadn't tried to contact him, even though he'd told her where he lived.

Confronting her was anything but pleasant. He put her on the defensive, though that hadn't been his intention. He wasn't sure he learned anything useful from meeting her again. They certainly hadn't patched things up, and he still didn't know how deeply she was involved in Kent's scheme. If she knew how he exploited the boys she was "helping" she didn't show it.

Maybe the phone number in San Francisco she'd provided would lead him to Kent—and to Debra.

CHAPTER 18

Lieutenant Pat Garrigan, armed with a subpoena, arrived at the main office of the Pacific Bell telephone company on Montgomery Street in San Francisco. He edged his way past a queue of protesting patrons, and approached the receptionist. A familiar figure stood before her. As he drew closer, he could detect anger in the young man's voice.

"Mallory?"

Blake turned abruptly. "Garrigan," he said. If he felt any great surprise, he hid it.

"You're a hard man to reach," Garrigan said. "You didn't return my calls."

"Didn't get any messages. I've been away from home for a while."

"May I ask where and why?"

"You may. But I won't answer unless I can see what it has to do with finding Debra."

Garrigan raised his eyebrows. "Come sit down." He looked around for a place that might provide some privacy. "In my car, if you don't mind. I have a lot of questions regarding the investigation."

"And lose my place in line?" Blake looked at people lined up behind him. "Maybe your questions could wait until I'm done here."

"Fair enough. I'll take care of my business, too, while we're here." Garrigan turned to the receptionist and handed her the subpoena. "I want the last six months' telephone bills for Debra Randall."

The brunette behind the desk looked up, mouth open, but when Garrigan flashed his badge, she nodded and went to a filing cabinet. "I'll make copies," she said.

"While you're at it, perhaps you can get the same for this number," Blake said, handing Garrigan the slip of paper Ellen had given him. When Garrigan hesitated, he added, "It concerns Debra."

Garrigan nodded, and when the receptionist came back with a folder, he handed it to her. "This number, too."

She frowned at Blake and then the line of patrons waiting for service but went after the requested files.

When she returned, Blake reached for the file, but Garrigan took it from the woman's hand, thanked her, and said to Blake, "Follow me to my office, and we'll discuss these files."

"How about the coffee shop across the street?" Blake said. "I'll meet you over there."

"Why?"

Blake said, "I'll explain when I meet you there, but I'm not leaving with you."

Blake walked around the block and entered from the alley.

"Okay, why the sneaking around?" Garrigan asked when they were seated at a corner table. "And why did you want the records for this number?" He waved the folder in front of Blake before opening it.

"I want to see whose name is on the bill and what calls were made. And I want the address for the phone."

"Where'd you get this number?" Garrigan asked as he opened the file.

"What difference does that make?"

Garrigan looked at the name on the bills. "Sam Smith." The name he'd heard from Paul. He looked up in surprise. "Do you know this guy?"

Blake sighed. "It's an alias for Kent Mallory." When Garrigan's eyes widened, Blake added, "Yes. He's my brother."

"There are calls to a number in Los Angeles, "Garrigan said, "and several to a number in British Columbia." He scrutinized Blake's face. "What do you make of it?"

"Kent lives in Canada. But I think he was here at approximately the time Debra disappeared. That's what I want to find out."

"Does any of this have to do with the manuscript you took from Miss Randall's desk drawer?"

Blake stared back hard but didn't answer.

"Something called *Canadian Odyssey*, I believe," Garrigan said. "Why did you take it?"

"It's personal. I knew Deb was writing something, and she said she'd let me read it, but I didn't know what it was. I took it to find out."

"Why is it personal, if she wrote it."

"It's about a trip we took."

"I want to see the manuscript," Garrigan said.

"I don't think so. Like I said, it's personal."

"We'll see about that. Now tell me, why didn't you come to me with information about these phone calls, about the manuscript, and anything else you're keeping to yourself?" Garrigan didn't try to conceal the anger he felt. "Do you want me to find her or not? If you do, quit withholding information that could help."

"I didn't come to you, because I don't want to put her in more danger than she's already in. I shouldn't be talking to you now. If Kent has someone spying on me, it could mean her life."

"Then I think you'd better tell me all you know. If she's in a life-or-death situation, the sooner we get to her the better. Am I right?"

"If he has her, as I believe, and he hears that I've gone to the police, he might decide to kill her rather than keep her alive to torture her, as he said he would."

"Then you'd better tell me what you know," Garrigan growled.

"Damn you!" Blake said. "If he has someone trailing me, the fact that I even spoke to you could put her in jeopardy."

"We're wasting time," Garrigan said, leaning closer. "Confound it, Mallory! If seeing you with me is putting her in danger, let me help save her before it's too late."

Shaking his head, Blake sighed. He told Garrigan about his brother's threat, and how local law enforcement was protecting him.

Garrigan listened intently without once jotting down a note, as Blake spilled all he knew. Blake finished by saying, "If Kent's not at this address, I'll fly to his plantation to see if he's there. If he is, I'll make him tell me where he's hiding Deb. Or die trying."

"Don't be foolish. We'll get the Mounties to raid his place, but first I'm going to the address for this phone number and see who's living there. If they are spies, or if it's your brother himself, I'll make some arrests."

"On what grounds?"

"Don't worry. I'll think of something to get him locked up long enough to get the RCMP to raid the place. You coming? I need you to identify your brother if he's there."

"Of course. That's why I'm here."

A young Vietnamese woman came to the door. "May I help you, please?" she asked.

"We're from the phone company," Garrigan said. "May we come in?"

"Yes. Of course." She stepped back and gestured for them to enter.

"Do you live here, Miss...?"

"My name is Amy Nyugen. Yes. This is my home. I live here for many years. I pay my rent on time."

"I'm sure you do. I just wondered who lives here with you."

"Nobody. I live by myself."

"But your phone number is listed in a different name."

"Oh, yes. But he does not live here. His name is Sammy Smith, and he lives in Canada with my sister, his wife."

"Why is the phone in his name?"

"When he comes to visit, he needs to have a telephone for business. He is a big businessman. He sells his fruit and vegetables all over the country. He needs a telephone so he had it hooked up. He supposed to pay the phone bill, not me."

"Does he come here often?"

"Yes. My sister, she likes to visit me, so he comes with her. He never used to come visit, but for many months they come often and stay sometimes a few days. Sometimes more than a week."

"Do you use the phone much?"

"Only to call my sister. But Sammy, he use it a lot whenever he comes."

"Was he here last month?" Blake asked.

"Yes, he stay long time, more than a week. Then he left my sister here, and we don't see him again for many days."

"Did you and your sister know where he went?" Garrigan asked.

"Why you want to know all this?"

"No reason. I just came to ask about the phone. We have orders to disconnect it, and I just wanted to make sure there was no mistake."

"Sammy wants it disconnected?"

"That's my understanding." Garrigan sounded convincing, even to Blake.

"Oh, he must think I talk too long to my sister. Sometimes we talk about him, but she says, 'Don't tell him.' Maybe he found out. I hope he is not mad at her."

"Why do you say that? Would he hurt her?"

"I do not know. He is a very sweet guy—except when he is angry. He has a bad temper, my sister says."

"Your sister's with him now?" Blake asked.

"Yes. He pick her up yesterday. He seem angry, so I don't want to cause him no trouble."

"Well, don't worry," Garrigan said. "We'll just take out the connection as he asked. It probably doesn't mean he's angry with your sister. Probably just a business decision."

"Okay. I will not worry, then."

"What did you do that for?" Blake asked after they left with the phone jack.

"I didn't want her to alert your brother. I don't think she knows what he's really up to, but this way she can't tell him we were here without going somewhere else—which she might do, so I think we best move quickly."

"What do you have in mind?"

"Can you find out if he's at his place in Canada?"

"Yes, I'll fly over it."

"I know some people with the Royal Canadian Mounted Police in British Columbia. I think when I tell them the situation, they'll raid his operation, but I don't want to go in there and find nothing."

"They'll find plenty."

"Then, I'll get a team ready to go as soon as I hear from you."

"You sure you can trust your Mountie friend? I know for a fact that Kent has help from a local policeman to make sure his men don't escape, and I have evidence that he's bought the cooperation of the Kelowna police. Why not the Mounties while he's at it?"

Garrigan frowned. "That's absurd. You can't buy the Canadian feds."

"Anyone can be bought if the price is right," Blake scoffed. "I'll fly up there first thing in the morning."

"Hold up there. I can't arrange this overnight. Won't a plane flying over make him suspicious?"

"Possibly. I don't think it's a regular airplane route. I'll stay high and off to the side. Just enough to see if his vehicles are there." Blake didn't want to take a chance that might let his brother escape. "How much time do you need?"

"Give me three days. I'll let you know when it's set," Garrigan insisted.

"Two tops, and even that might be too late."

Once in his plane, Blake strongly considered flying north instead of back to Texas. Kent could be raping and torturing Debra right now. What if he couldn't stop him? He imagined confronting his brother in a gun fight. Or worse, Kent holding a gun to Debra's head, and once again, he would be helpless. Now that Garrigan and the RCMP were involved, he'd have to go along with their plan to take him by surprise. He'd have to wait. He felt like a coward, though, as he banked the plane and headed southeast.

CHAPTER 19

Blake couldn't sleep. He tried to keep busy, but no activity could clear the worry from his mind. When he finally fell asleep the second night home, he was tortured by nightmares in which his mother, dressed in black leather, snapped a whip in the air and cheered Kent on as he attacked Debra. He couldn't see Debra's face clearly in the dream, but her body was bruised and bloody and stretched out on a bed with chains. He awakened, cold, shaking, and soaked in sweat. He called Garrigan.

"I'm going now, ready or not."

"Give me one more day," Garrigan said. "Don't mess this up now, Mallory."

Blake serviced his plane and flew to British Columbia. Fearing that Kent or one of his goons would recognize his Cessna, he rented a Piper PA 25 Pawnee crop duster and flew over Kent Mallory's mountain plantation. He noticed a flurry of activity, he wished he could see better. But he didn't dare fly back over the area at a lower altitude and raise suspicion. He noted that Kent's Jeep, VW bus, and his car were all there, as well as a semi-trailer loaded with hay bales. That was all he needed to know. Or at least he hoped so.

He returned to Kelowna and called Garrigan. "I'm in Kelowna. Kent's there, at least for now. Where are you? I've rented a car and am ready to go."

"I'll be there first thing in the morning. Meet me at the airport."

"Damn it, Garrigan, are you waiting for Kent to get

word, take Debra, and run or kill her and hide her body?"

"Don't go without me. I'll be there."

Blake didn't like it, but at this point, it would be foolish to go without Garrigan and Canadian law enforcement. He got a hamburger, drove to the edge of town to eat it, but tossed most of it to the begging ducks. He grew cold, standing there, so he walked. Walked and thought. Had he made a huge mistake leveling with Garrigan? Not that he thought Garrigan was anything but legit, but he didn't like the Canadian feds being pulled in. But this was Canada, so what could he do? He finally drove back to the airport, found a more or less comfortable seat, pulled his hat over his eyes, and slept. It was a long night, but the lawmen finally arrived.

When they were on the way, Blake driving, Frank, the Mountie, in the back seat and Garrigan riding shotgun, Garrigan said, "The RCMP has a chopper ready to take off from Kelowna. They'll give us a head start so we get there at about the same time. When we get to the gravel road, you say is about five or six miles from his house, Frank will give the signal to his Emergency Response Team to 'drop in on him.'"

Frank chuckled.

Blake didn't see anything funny. He wished he hadn't taken Garrigan into his confidence.

"We want to take him by surprise, so we'll hold back until the chopper lands," Garrigan said.

As Blake drove in, he noticed the semi load of hay was gone. He parked behind Kent's Jeep. Four men, dressed in dark jackets, helmets, and with guns drawn were jumping from the white chopper marked "Police."

Kent sauntered out of his house—smiling.

"Yo! To what do I owe the honor of a visit from our country's honorable Royal Police?" he asked.

"We have a warrant for your arrest and to search your premises," Frank said, as he strode to meet Kent. "Put your arms in the air."

"Arrest? For what?" Kent raised both arms.

"Drug trafficking to begin with."

"What makes you think I have drugs? Did my baby brother tell you that crazy story?" Kent smirked at Blake.

"You lying son of a bitch!" Blake strode toward his brother, but Garrigan grabbed his arm.

Blake yelled, "Where is Debra? If you've hurt her, I'll kill you."

"Debra? Your girlfriend?" Kent frowned and shook his head. "If you've lost your girlfriend, don't blame me. She probably just moved on to someone better than you, punk!"

Blake broke loose from Garrigan's grip and lunged at Kent. "Where is she?"

Two of the Emergency Responders pushed Blake back, and Frank, with no hint of his former congenial manner, growled, "You'll let me take care of this. One more word or move out of you, and you can sit in the car."

A string of obscenities flowed through Blake's mind, but he only nodded as he burned with humiliation and rage.

"Now," Frank said, turning to Kent. "Keep your hands up." He nodded to two of his men who stepped forward to frisk him. They pulled a hand gun from Kent's waist band and a knife sheathed at his ankle.

"Why the arms?" Frank asked.

"You never know when you'll encounter a bear or lion in this country. I always stay prepared."

"All right. We need to take a look inside your green houses and out buildings. Then you can lead us to the marijuana field, though I don't suppose there is much to see this time of year. I'll need a shovel."

"What? Did Blakey tell you I grow marijuana? Last I knew that was illegal. That poor boy's delusional. You might want to get him psychiatric help. You saw him. He's seriously dangerous."

Damn, Kent's a good actor, Blake thought. But then he always was the biggest, most convincing liar he'd ever known. *He wants me to take his bait,* Blake thought, but he didn't speak. Once inside the greenhouses and the labs, the authorities would know the truth.

That didn't happen.

The green houses were mostly empty but for a few potted flowers in one and a half-dozen tomato plants in the other. The lab where Blake was sure Kent made or processed meth smelled of fresh paint. Only a table with some art supplies and an easel stood in the middle of the room.

"My wife's studio. Not all of her work is here, as we took it off the walls to repaint. She decided she wanted it white to give her work more light."

Blake's hopes plummeted. Kent had been forewarned. If only he'd carried out his various schemes instead of leveling with Garrigan. His thoughts went back to the plans he'd debated on: sneak into Kent's room in the middle of the night and slit his throat? Fly in with a gun and hope to win in a shootout? Hike in, hide and wait for a chance to shoot him? He was favoring the latter when he'd met Garrigan at the telephone office. Not that he'd ever killed a man, but if it would save Debra, he'd do it. Even if it meant life in prison or the gas chamber. Garrigan's plan had the appeal that they might find her without his having to commit the crime. All scenarios, including this one, ended with him searching for Debra, finding her and releasing her. *She's here somewhere,* he was sure of it. *The drugs and the men may have been removed, but maybe Debra's alive.*

"How deep is the snow in the field," Garrigan asked, looking at the banks piled by the driveway.

"Deep," Kent said. "Almost bare a week or so ago, but then we got this typical early-March snowstorm.

"I don't think it's worth digging through the snow for a soil sample," Frank said. "Nothing else has been as described."

"You wouldn't find much," Kent offered. "We plowed the oat straw under after we harvested last fall."

"There's the house and one more building to look through," Frank said, "Might as well look at everything while we're here." He cast a disgruntled look at Blake. What an embarrassing disappointment this would be if their search turned up nothing.

Kent shook his head ruefully, saying, "The guest house. I don't like to barge in on the privacy of clients."

His men are locked in the bunkhouse, Blake thought, his hopes rising again.

"Sorry, but you'll have to let us in," Frank said.

"I rent out this building as a hostel for people wanting to go hiking or rock climbing in the hills," Kent explained. "A group of five guys have it rented for the week,

117

but I think they're off looking for ice-climbing sites right now. Could you wait until they return?"

"No, we can't. Open it."

Kent fumbled for the key and unlocked the door. The large room, lined with cots along each wall, a table and chairs in the center, a kitchenette on the far end, was empty other than some clothing strewn across chairs and the floor. There was nothing else, as the search quickly revealed.

The house, though neat and clean and furnished just as Blake remembered it, was deserted. "My wife Millie is visiting her sister in San Francisco for a week. Sorry she's not here to greet you and offer you some tea and cookies," Kent said, smirking. "I'm not much of a cook, myself."

Really? Blake wondered. *We were there just three days ago.*

"There must be a cellar. An attic, maybe." Blake said, frantically. "Debra!" he shouted. "DEBRA, where are you?"

Garrigan grabbed his arm and squeezed it. Frank asked Kent if he had a basement, which Kent swore he did not. "Let's have a look at the attic access, then."

Blake was grateful that Frank was listening to him.

Kent got a ladder and made a big production of climbing up and opening an access door in the hallway ceiling and inviting Frank to climb up and look. He even handed Frank a flashlight.

"Nothing there," Frank finally conceded. "I guess I owe you an apology, sir."

"I'm staying," Blake declared. "I know she's here. I just hope it's not in a grave. But if it is, I'll find it."

"No, you're not," Kent growled. "You are not welcome on my property. Now get off, and don't come back!"

"What have you done to Debra, Kent?"

"Not a damned thing. I don't know where she is. I hope this isn't a big production to cover up what you might have done with her. How about it, Blake, did you kill her?"

Blake lunged at him again, but Garrigan restrained him and shoved him into the back seat of the car.

Frank drove back in silence. Blake could almost see steam coming from his ears.

"Well, that's the most I've ever been embarrassed in all the years I've been working in law enforcement," Garrigan groused. "I'm sorry Frank. Blake had me convinced."

"Can't you see? He was warned," Blake pleaded. "I told you he owned law enforcement. He had time to hide everything before we got there. I'd like to know who told him."

Both Frank and Garrigan remained stone faced and silent.

CHAPTER 20

Blake felt like a fool, but he wouldn't give up. He'd wait a day or two, and then he'd go back. He believed that Kent would soon have his men busy starting new plants in the green houses, where they must have destroyed some to hide evidence. Never again would he trust law enforcement to do a job he should have done a long time ago. In the meantime, he'd finish Deb's diary.

> Not until I was cleared for takeoff and in the air at cruising altitude, did I take time to look at Blake. What I saw terrified me. His face, twisted in pain, was ashen, the bruises around his eye, bright purple, green, and black. The cut on his forehead gaped open, encrusted with dried blood, and oozing a pink liquid. He slipped in and out of consciousness, muttering unintelligibly.
>
> "I'm going to land at Sea-Tac," I told him, not sure he was conscious enough to understand. "I've got to get you to a hospital."
>
> "No, no, keep going. I just want to get home."
>
> "But," I began, but he interrupted me.
>
> "I'll see a doctor in LA. I don't think a few more hours will make much difference."
>
> "You sure?"
>
> "Yeah," he said, sounding determined. "Your dad is going to be furious if his plane isn't back pronto." Clenching his teeth against pain, he added. "Don't tell him about Kent, though."

"No, I won't. I've thought of that. I don't want Dad involved."

"I've got to thank your father for building comfortable seats." Blake's attempt at a smile looked more like a ghoulish grimace. He saw my hesitation and ordered, "Keep going."

He seemed to fall asleep until we hit some turbulence over northern California. He woke with cries of pain. His face had a green tinge.

"This is nonsense. I'm not waiting for you to die before I get you medical help. We're landing in San Francisco."

"Okay," he said, gritting his teeth.

I radioed ahead for an ambulance to meet us at the airport.

X-rays showed that three of his ribs were broken, his upper arm splintered, and the bones in his wrist shattered. His blood pressure was dangerously low, and they told me he could be bleeding internally. If he died, I would forever blame myself for not getting him to a hospital sooner.

"We need to operate as soon as possible, but first we have to start a blood transfusion," the ER doctor told me.

"Do you have blood? I'll give him mine, if it matches."

But my blood didn't match. "Don't worry," they said. "We have his type in the blood bank."

I stayed by his side as they got blood flowing into his good arm and finally took him to the operating room. "He'll be in surgery for three to four hours, at the very least," the doctor said.

I paced the floor waiting for news. "Kent,
I'll kill you with my bare hands if Blake dies," I
swore, garnering startled looks from others in
the waiting room. I wondered if Kent was alive.
Could he have survived the collision with the
truck? I think it would be a miracle if either he
or the cop survived, but I thought if he's alive,
he should be arrested, and that local cop along
with him. With that in mind, I went in search
of a pay phone, called information for the
number, and put in a call to the Kelowna Police
Department.

"I want to report a big marijuana farm in
the mountains above your city. The owner is
using draft dodgers from the U.S. to grow his
crop. He has them imprisoned."

"What is your name and where are you calling from?" the voice on the phone asked after a
moment's hesitation.

"That doesn't matter. I think the men he has
working for him are in danger. I spoke to one of
them, and he told me the owner won't let them
leave. I think he may have murder..."

"I'm sorry, ma'am, but I need to get your
information first so I can file your complaint.
Did you see this marijuana farm you're telling
me about?"

"Yes."

"Your name, please, and the number you are
calling from.

I slammed the phone receiver down, my
heart beating fast. It was a mistake to call.
What if Kent didn't get killed in the crash and

they trace the call and tell him where we are?'
I needed to get Blake to LA or back to Texas
before that could happen. I just hoped he'd live
through surgery.

I paced the hallways, trying to formulate
a plan. Passing the pay phone again, I decided to call Paul. I wanted to hear his voice, to
spill my troubles to my best friend, but I knew
I shouldn't get him involved. Well, I could at
least hear his voice.

"Hello?" The feminine voice threw me off.

"Hello, hello. Anyone there?" she repeated.

"Uh, sorry. Maureen? I was calling for Paul."

Paul came on right away.

"Debra? Where are you? Are you okay?"

"Yes, I'm fine. I'm in San Francisco with
some time to kill, so I thought I'd say hi. If
you're busy..."

"No, not too busy to talk to you. Too bad you
didn't have time to kill on Sunday. We missed
you at the wedding."

"Wedding?" I asked, mystified. "What wedding?"

"My wedding, Debra. I thought you'd be
there, being my best friend and all."

"But, Paul, I didn't know when it was. Why
didn't you tell me?"

"We sent you an invitation three weeks ago."

"I must not have gotten it. I'm so sorry, you
know I would have come."

"Debra, you sent back the RSVP."

"No, Paul. Someone else must have."

"It sure looks like your handwriting. It just
says, 'I'll try.'"

"Paul, I'm so sorry. It's been crazy. It would have been impossible, anyway, as it turned out, but if I'd known... I just got in from Canada, and I couldn't have made it back any sooner."

I wracked my brain for a memory of the invitation. For a split second, I thought I remembered, but then the image was gone. If I'd seen an invitation, I'd remember. My best friend's wedding? It would be huge in my mind. True, I didn't approve of Paul's choice of brides, but I'd still support him.

"So where are you now?" Paul asked.

"I'm at the hospital. Blake's in surgery. He went with me to Kelowna and was in an accident."

"How? Where?"

I was trying to think of a good lie, when Paul questioned me. "If he was hurt in Canada, why is he here?"

"It's a long story," I said, flustered. "Look. I'm sorry. I shouldn't have bothered you. Tell Maureen I'm sorry I couldn't make it to your wedding. I'm sure it was beautiful."

I plunked down the phone, confused and deflated. Maybe Maureen just told him she'd sent the invitation. She has always hated me. Then she forged a reply. That had to be it.

I couldn't sit still. Blake would be in surgery for at least a couple more hours and then another in recovery. I decided to leave a message at the nurse's station to tell Blake I'd be back in the evening or tomorrow morning at the latest. "And no visitors, please. Don't give out his room number. He doesn't want to see anyone

but me." I hoped that was enough to keep him
safe if Kent came looking for him. I needed to
get the Raptor back to Dad's plant, get my own
plane, and come back for Blake.

It was past closing time, all the employees
were gone by the time I got to LA, and Dad was
waiting for me when I got out of the Raptor.
    "Where the hell have you been? Why
weren't you at Paul's wedding? I hope you
have a damned good excuse."
    I felt six years old, again, cowed by my
father's angry voice. "I went to Canada. You
knew that. You said I could take the..."
    "You didn't say when. I never dreamed
you'd take off the weekend of Paul's wedding.
Harry was offended, and Mattie is sick with
worry. Call them." He turned and stomped
back to the main building, evidently not at all
interested in my explanation. As usual.
    What a day! It was dark by the time I got
to my apartment. I shed my clothes, stepped
into the shower, and stood under the pounding
stream until the water ran cold. By the time I
dressed, I was exhausted. I doubted I'd make
two blocks without falling asleep. I decided I'd
better stay home for the night and trust the
hospital to take care of Blake.
    First, I'd call Mattie. I leaned over my desk,
picked up the phone, and dialed Mattie's number. As I waited for it to go through, I moved a
newspaper—uncovering a gold-embossed envelope. I fell into my chair and dropped the phone
into its cradle.

As I stared at the engraved invitation, the memory came back, piece by piece. What the hell was wrong with my mind? Sure, Paul had told me he was getting married, but I didn't expect it to be so soon. Had I known when? The invitation nudged my memory. I remembered being upset when I read it. Staring at the envelope, I began to see myself take the RSVP card and scribble on it. I fastened it to the mailbox outside with a clothespin. How had I forgotten that? It's like it wasn't me. I clutched my crystal prism, pulling it from beneath my clean blouse. I think I did the same thing after mailing the card. The memory and reality coincided with a crash as a "feeling" began to overwhelm me. I heard the roar, I saw the ripples. And just as I had on the day, I got the invitation, I stumbled to the bedroom, crawled into bed, and pulled the covers over my head.

CHAPTER 21

Blake put the manuscript—or rather, the diary—down, his emotions in chaos. He wanted to understand Deb's spells. To help her. How she must love Paul, to be so upset by his marriage. He'd tried so hard to get over the jealousy he'd always felt toward Paul. There was no doubt that Debra adored, respected, and looked up to him as the problem solver in her life. She loved him *like a big brother*, or so she said. Yet Blake felt that Paul was the standard he was held to, and he had to measure up in order to have Debra's respect.

Oh God, what's wrong with me? Blake moaned. *If I can just find you in time to save your life, my love, I'll leave you alone, if that's what you want. I just want to know you're okay. And I'm pretty sure you're not.*

When he picked up the diary to continue reading, he groaned, seeing it was about a time he'd much rather forget.

December 30, 1970

It was not my intention to be in California for Christmas, let alone the apartment I'd mostly abandoned. Never again will I let Maureen or anyone else manipulate my family like this. And she's not even here! Christmas was always my favorite holiday, one that was always celebrated with the whole family, including Paul and his parents in the big house on our

127

ranch. And from now on, it always will be.

Blake had noticed the sparks flying between Debra and Paul, that night, especially when she asked for a rum and coke. He couldn't imagine why, but found out soon enough. She got sick during dinner, ran to the bathroom to throw up. Everyone finished without her, but it had been a quiet meal after that. When finished, Blake excused himself and went looking for her. She'd crashed on the bed in the spare room of her apartment. He spoke to her, but couldn't rouse her.

Paul came in and tried to awaken her to say goodbye. "Kitten," he'd said. "If you can hear me, your Dad and Ann said to tell you goodnight. I'm leaving, too. But I'll check on you in the morning. Mom and Dad have gone, but said to give you their love."

Debra didn't respond, and Blake suggested they call a doctor.

"She'll be all right once she sleeps it off. Probably brought on one of her..." Paul didn't finish whatever he was going to say, but started over. "If you can, stay with her. She's going to have a doozy of a headache when she wakes up."

"What's wrong with her?"

"She's allergic to alcohol. She should've known better. She was mad at me for letting Maureen spoil her plan to have Christmas at the ranch. I guess she thought she was getting even with me. Damn, she can be stubborn, and now she's the one paying for it."

It turned out much worse than her waking with a headache. Blake had never been so confused, hurt, and angry in his life. When she finally seemed awake and lucid, he'd showered, dressed, and confronted her before leaving her apartment and her life. And though he'd rather forget that Christmas and the days that followed, he picked up the diary and relived it all again from her perspective.

When I came out of the bathroom, Blake was sitting on the bed, fully dressed.

Debra," he said. "I just want to know what's happening. You told me about your migraines. My mother had migraines, and when she did, she lay in bed with her eyes covered and never moved. She didn't get up and roam around muttering to herself."

"I did that?" Alarmed, I sat next to him. "Please tell me what I did, what I said."

"You don't know?"

"No."

"That's damned scary, Debra."

"I know."

"You got up and didn't know who I was. You wanted to go out, but I didn't let you. I told you Kent could be out there, and you asked, 'Who's Kent?' You seemed drunk, but I knew you hadn't had but a few swallows of rum and Coke."

"I don't remember any of that. Did you bring me back up to the loft and put me to bed?"

"Hardly. When I blocked the door, you turned and ran upstairs. I started to follow but you said, 'Stay,' like you were talking to a dog. You acted afraid of me, so I stayed downstairs."

I couldn't believe what he was telling me. Was he making things up, an excuse to leave

129

me? I never really thought so. Blake is the most honest man I've ever met.

I was astonished at the mess my room was in. My jeans, shirt, and underclothes were scattered across the floor; my dress was on the bed. Open drawers spilled clothing over the rims and onto the floor. I'm normally neat as a pin and couldn't imagine dropping my clothes and leaving them. I must have had a terrible, drunken nightmare and acted it out in my sleep.

"My room's such a mess. How in heck did this happen?" I asked Blake, ready to accuse him.

"I don't know. It was like this when I came up to check on you and take a shower." He looked me in the eyes and asked, "Is this your usual reaction to alcohol?"

"I don't know. I don't normally drink."

"So, tell me this. When you said you have migraines, is this what you were talking about?"

"I didn't know how to describe what I get," I said. "Migraines seemed close enough because I don't get them very often. I thought they were getting better, but this has to be the worst one I've ever had, probably because of the alcohol. I don't know what it is other than a feeling I get sometimes. A really weird feeling. And—I lose time."

"Do you hear voices?" Blake's tone bordered on mocking.

"I hear a voice." If he was going to write me off as crazy, I might as well tell it all.

"I don't know, Debra. This might be just a little too weird for me. I need some time to think." He picked up his bag.

"Where are you going?"

"Home. I've already wasted too much time away from work."

I followed him downstairs, hoping he'd change his mind.

When the door closed behind him, I picked up my shriveled orchid and hurled it at the door. "I'm a waste of time, am I? Well damn you. You can go to hell." I slumped to the floor and sobbed, wishing him not in hell, but back in my arms.

Blake felt like a complete failure. Why had he ever thought he could forget her? Why hadn't he delved into the illness or whatever it was she was suffering instead of running away? Whether Kent had kidnapped her or she had succumbed to one of her spells, he felt responsible. And he had to find out.

He stuffed the diary in a drawer, vowing not to look at it again until he figured out something he could do to save her. Go back to Canada? Get Kent to tell him where he had Debra hidden before he killed him? Yeah, sure. He didn't think the chances of winning that battle were in his favor. And that made him feel more like a coward than ever.

He went to the hangar and worked furiously on dismantling an airplane that had been sitting in need of repair for more than a month. He ignored the ringing phone, put up a sign over the office door. "Closed for maintenance."

Hard work filled his days and nights until he was too exhausted to keep working. He could keep his mind busy this way until forced to sleep. Or try to. He'd barely get to sleep before another nightmare where his mother was involved in Debra's persecution would jolt him awake.

This is nonsense. If my mother is involved, I need to know it. Maybe she knows where Kent's hiding her.

He fueled his Cessna and headed for Los Angeles.

Ellen was shocked when Blake stomped into the little restaurant and demanded that she level with him.

"I don't know what you're talking about, Blake Mallory. What on earth?"

"We have to talk," he said.

"Give me a minute," she said. "It's been a slow day, and I was about to close up."

He paced until she gathered her things and locked the front door. "Come to my place," she said, "and tell me what on earth is wrong."

"Do you know where Kent has Debra? Is she dead or alive?"

"Debra? What do you mean? You think Kent has something to do with her disappearance?"

"I think he has everything to do with it. And I want you to tell me the truth. Tell me everything you know about him."

"I don't know what you're accusing me of, but it better not be lying. I have never told you or anyone else a lie. It's one thing I can't abide. You should know that."

"How should I know that, Mother? From the way you *didn't* tell me you were leaving me when I was thirteen years old?"

"Leaving you was wrong. I told you I regretted it. But

I didn't lie. What is it you think I'm keeping from you now?"

"Your involvement in Kent's whole operation. Did you help him get the money to buy the ranch in Canada for his drug trade?"

"Drug trade? What makes you think he's into that. He raises cattle, wheat, oats, and vegetables. I can show you pictures. And, yes, I cosigned a loan for him to buy property, but he paid it all back."

"So that you would send him men to work his marijuana fields and meth labs?"

"Blake. I know you don't get along with your brother, but accusing him of such things when he has turned his life around is going too far. You should go visit him and see for yourself."

"Have you ever done that? When was the last time you visited his place?"

"I haven't. But I have been in touch with him. He calls once every month or so to see how I'm doing. He asked me about Debra, not long after she quit flying for me. He was sincerely sympathetic when I told him her doctors said she couldn't fly anymore because of her headaches."

Blake remembered he'd suggested that ruse after their Canadian encounter, because they didn't know how closely Ellen was tied to Kent's operation. He'd also helped her move out of her LA apartment, because Ellen knew where she lived, and they feared she'd tell Kent.

"Well, I have been there. I flew with Debra on the last flight, met Kent, and went to his place because Deb wanted to check on her boys. When we saw what Kent didn't want us to see, we barely escaped with our lives. And he threatened to torture and kill her."

Ellen collapsed into a chair, all the color gone from her face. "Tell me, Son. How could I have misjudged him? I just wanted to believe he'd turned out all right."

Blake told her everything, watching for any tell-tale signs that she was lying. None came. She cried, sobbing just as hard as she had the night before she left him when he was a teenager. She got up, went to her bedroom, and came back with a shoe box, secured with a rubber band. Opening it, she showed Blake the letters Kent had written to her, regaling her with descriptions of his ranch with crops of wheat, oats, alfalfa, and cattle. He'd sent her pictures of greenhouses full of flowers and tomato plants, and farms and ranches that were not his.

"I'm so sorry, I didn't know. You must go to the police and tell them."

"I tried that. Kent was forewarned and hid everything. The Royal Canadian Mounted Police and the City of San Francisco will never believe me again. I'm relieved that it wasn't you who alerted him."

"You thought...?"

"I didn't know what to think, but I can't tell you how glad I am to find out you didn't know what Kent was doing." Blake hugged her. With her head on his chest, she hugged back, taking him back to memories of the kind, caring mother he had loved with all his heart when he was young.

After visiting his mother, Blake could not sit still. He had to go back and look for Debra. Flying high over the mountains above Kelowna, Blake noticed something he hadn't before. High above Kent's alfalfa field, was a small clearing with a narrow path leading away from it.

He flew back to Kelowna, rented a car and drove toward Kent's place. He took the gravel road and continued on past Kent's driveway three or four miles until a snow drift kept him from going farther. From there he walked.

It took an hour to find the clearing he'd seen from the sky, and the small, but fairly new structure in it. A small building, perfectly square, with a window on one side and a door on the other. He tried the doorknob and was surprised that it was not locked. The single room had a wood-burning stove in the middle of it, a few cabinets and counter tops on one side. Another lab? The shelves and cupboards were empty.

Blake pounded on the floor. It sounded hollow. A place to hide Debra? A body? He pounded the floor, got on his hands and knees and yelled her name. Did he hear something? He wasn't sure. He lay with his ear to the floor and shouted again. Nothing. He was about to get up when he noticed a crack between the stone hearth and the floor. It was a good quarter inch, and not caulked.

He looked under the stove and found a metal vent cover, decorative steel about a foot long and four inches wide. Looking further, he found a latch, securing the hearth to the floor.

Once he released the latch, and plied his weight to the stove, hearth and all pivoted out of the way, revealing a hole with a ladder descending into the darkness. He climbed down.

CHAPTER 22

"Debra?" he asked softly? "Deb!" A little louder. "Sweet-heart, can you hear me? Are you here?"

It was so damned dark; he couldn't see a thing past the ladder. The silence made him shiver. He did not want to find her dead. He knocked something off a shelf as he felt his way. Sweeping the floor with his hand, he grasped a cold metal cylinder. He found a switch and pressed it. A circle of light illuminated the room. What he saw brought bile to his mouth. A double bed, covered with a soft, white blanket and new fluffy pillows, had six-feet high posts at each corner. Four rails ran across the top between them, lengthwise. Four chains ending in leather straps, made to buckle around wrists and ankles, hung from them. Hanging on the walls of the room were various tools of torture, many of which Blake could only guess their purpose.

He explored every inch of the room, going so far as to crawl under the bed looking for any sign of a break in the concrete floor where a body could be buried. He ex-plored every corner and cupboard only to find more sex toys and instruments of torture, as well as some sexy lin-gerie, with tags still attached, novels, puzzle books, and even a teddy bear. None of it looked used.

Debra definitely wasn't here. That was somewhat of a relief, as he'd been so afraid of finding her dead.

Maybe Kent had captured her, planning to bring her here, but she'd resisted. Of course, she'd resist. She'd fight like a cornered tiger as long as she had breath, so

Kent had been forced to kill her. Was she buried somewhere on the property? He put the hearth back in place and left the building. Even though there were definite signs of spring in the valley, April snow lay deep on the ground here, covering any signs of previous activity. It didn't matter. She was dead. Finding the room without her in it convinced him.

Back in Marfa, Blake went into hiding, grieving, in the privacy of his tiny room in the loft over the office attached to the hangar. He alternately sobbed and slept, sleeping deeply and dreamlessly, only to awaken to the reality of the aching empty hole in his life and the shame of not being man enough to save her. Time passed without his noticing or caring.

At last, he decided that since he could not forget her, he'd read her last words, perhaps they'd tell him what he needed to know. He went down to his office, dug out the diary pages, and found the place where he'd left off.

The phone rang. Blake had no interest in answering. It finally stopped after ten rings. *Good,* he thought.

Almost immediately, it rang again. Annoyed, Blake crossed to where it sat on the desk, picked up the receiver and slammed it back down. Two seconds later, it rang again.

This time he answered to a voice so loud he pulled the phone from his ear and still heard it plainly.

"Who the hell do you think you are, withholding information that could save her? If she dies, it's on you, man. I hope you can live with yourself..."

"Hello, Paul."

"Blake, why didn't you tell us about your brother? Garrigan called me yesterday to say they are closing the

137

case. He said you knew about a guy named Kent Mallory's threat to kill her. Damn you for not telling us."

Blake said nothing. He couldn't blame Paul for being outraged, and he wasn't surprised that Garrigan had told him. He'd probably hear from Josh next. *Closed the case, huh. Just as well.* It had closed for him the day he found the torture chamber Kent had made for her.

"I'd like to wring your neck, but first I want to read the manuscript you've been keeping to yourself. What right do you have to do that?"

"Telling would have put her in more danger, Paul."

"Like hell. If we'd known, we could have protected her!"

"How? By going to the police? She didn't want that. Kent had the police in his hands. That's how he knew I was coming with Garrigan and the Mounties in time to hide everything." *Maybe that was how. Or Millie's sister, Amy. Or maybe Kent's spies had seen him talking to Garrigan.*

"Garrigan thinks your brother was telling the truth," Paul said, his voice softening. "He said he thought you were right until he went there and found nothing like what was described in the manuscript, which he read and I want to see. Garrigan thinks it's just a novel, now that he's seen your brother's property."

"You want to read it, you'll have to come here. But it's not a manuscript for a novel. It's a diary—a true story."

"I'll charter a plane and be there in the morning. You'd better be there."

"I'll be here."

Blake was reading when Paul arrived. He handed him

all but the last several pages. He didn't have the heart to tell Paul that Debra was dead. He closed his eyes to hold back tears, his body sagging. He finally opened them and resumed reading.

He looked up when he heard a gasp. Paul's face was paper-white as he read the part about the assault. He'd cursed Blake more than once for not sharing information or going to the police. He did so again.

"Paul. I told you, Kent owned the police, not only the local cops, but the city cops too. Debra figured that out when she tried to report him to the Kelowna police. There was only one way to protect Debra. And I tried."

"What?"

Paul's attitude changed when Blake told him about going after Kent with a gun. "And I'm not done yet. Now that I know he's there, I will go back. I may be too late to save her, but I'll kill him or be killed trying. I don't care what happens to me. My life's shit without her."

"If you care so much, why did you break up with her. It just about broke her heart when she found out you were involved with another woman."

"What?"

"She didn't know if it was a girlfriend or a wife you were with, but she saw you when she went to Marfa to research her mother's history. She was going to eat at the café before driving home, but when she saw you with a beautiful, *extremely* friendly woman, she left. She said it was obvious that you were intimate."

"There has never been any woman but Debra." Blake frowned, thinking. "She must have seen me with a client. I agreed to have lunch with a woman who wanted me to fly her to Mexico with her fiancé and wouldn't take no

139

for an answer. I had to get quite rude to convince her I wasn't going to break promises to other clients in order to suit her schedule."

"But you did break up with Deb."

"Yeah, I thought it was best for both of us, if she was going to lie to me about her illness. She never even told me about her allergy to alcohol. That and her spells. I just read about her seizures or blackouts, or whatever those monsters were that she called her feelings." Blake pointed to the pages in his hand. "If only she'd told me. I wish I hadn't left her like that, but it was because she wouldn't trust me."

"But, you knew her life was still in danger."

"Yes, but how could I protect her? I begged her to come back to Texas where she'd be safe. She refused. I couldn't just close down my airport to stand guard. She could have come to her dad's ranch, but she insisted on staying in California."

Paul nodded. "Yeah, I guess I'll have to quit blaming you." He returned to the manuscript.

Blake picked up the few pages left and read on. Not that he hoped to find a new clue to her disappearance, but maybe he could find out what he might have done to save her. He read on.

I knew I needed to get out of the apartment. Go back into hiding. I promised myself I would, but first I had to get rid of the headache. I don't dare drive when my head hurts so badly, I can't see straight. I took four aspirin and went to my room. I woke up hours later, feeling better, though weak—even weaker than usual. I would have to have the worst "feeling" ever when Blake was here to see it. I still shake with

140

fear when I think of the things he said I did. Am I schizo? How many times have I gotten up and walked around, did things without knowing what I was doing? Maybe by keeping this diary, keeping track of every single minute of the day, I can find out.

If Kent gets hold of it, I'm dead, though. Yet I can't throw it away. I keep it tucked under reams of typing paper. I wish I could show it to Blake, but I'm doing my best to forget him. If he can't accept me as I am...Damn. I thought he was the one. Will I ever find a guy who can love me for what I am, not just for my looks and money?

And just what are you, Debra Randall? Who are you? Without my looks and money is there anything left to love? Just a very sick woman, if everything he told me about my unconscious behavior is true. I will avoid all men, especially Blake, until I figure myself out.

CHAPTER 23

The words felt like a stab to his heart, but he deserved them, he told himself. With just a few pages remaining, he had to keep reading. The next entry was made nearly a year ago.

June, 1971 (I guess I should put in a date occasionally, especially since it's been so long since I've written, in case it would be helpful to whomever finds it when I'm gone. So much for writing every day!)

I ended up staying in my San Francisco apartment at first. I wanted to go to the ranch for a while, but there wasn't time to go home before I was expected back at work. I merely unplugged my phone, made sure I didn't let any light shine out of my windows after dark, and left my car parked. I wear my wig and dark glasses whenever I leave the building, and always by the back door. Mostly, since I learned that Kent knows where I live—getting that horrible pornographic card at my home address—I stay in other places, but no one place too long.

I have no real reason to believe that Kent Mallory is no longer a threat, but I haven't heard a word from him since the first of the year. No more threatening letters to this address or even to the newspaper, so I've become less cautious and moved back in. I'm tired of letting men—especially that man—control my life. I've had no recent threats from him, so I think he may have given up.

The news tonight has left me livid. I'm more than furious at Nixon for keeping Johnson's war going. Killing for profit! Old men in suits sacrificing American boys for glory. I sat at my typewriter and, spurred by anger, typed out an article I feel is some of the best writing I'd ever done. I took it to my boss, and he turned it down. "A little too provocative for us, Debra. You should know that."

I stopped at Paul's office and tapped on the door.

His face lit up when he saw me. "What's up, Kitten."

"Got time to step out for a minute and get a cup of coffee with me?"

"Sure. I always have time for you." He grabbed his jacket.

We sat in the back booth of our favorite coffee shop, and I reached for his hand. "Paul, I want you to forgive me for my bad behavior last Christmas. I was a brat. I had a little rum just to spite you. Besides getting sick, I had the worst one of my 'feelings' ever. Made a terrible ass of myself..."

"Shhh," he said, "You don't have to apologize to me. Just don't quit being my friend."

"Thank you." I laid my article on the table between us. A President's Broken Promise

"What's this?" he asked.

"Nixon campaigned on the promise to end the draft. The blood of thousands of young men he forced to go be slaughtered in Vietnam is on his hands."

"Yeah?" Paul raised an eyebrow. He's heard me rant like this before.

"He could have ended the draft long ago. The military had no objection to it. Nixon set up a commission to examine it, a further delay, an excuse for him not to keep his promise. The commission came up with an answer in February, saying there is adequate military strength with volunteers. We don't need conscription. But did Nixon act on it? No, not right away.

Finally, it was scheduled to end this month, on June 30. But will Nixon let it? No. The liar. He's asked congress to approve a two-year extension. You know they will. How many more boys who don't want to be there will die in the meantime?"

Paul reached across the table to wipe tears from my cheek. "I'm sorry, Kitten," he said.

I did my best to compose myself and said. "I still can't figure out why in hell we work for this stodgy newspaper. I'm sick of getting my pieces turned down. I'm tired of watering down my political views to suit Dallas Steele's imaginary conservative readers."

"Not imaginary." He picked up the article and read. "God, this is good, Kitten. Send it to the Times or the Chronicle."

"I will. I'm ready to quit the Examiner."

"Don't quit, Kitten. I don't know what I'd do if you left town."

"It's time I do something for myself."

"Like what?"

"Like researching my own history. Find out who I am. I'm an investigative reporter. I should be able to find out who my mother was, how she died, and...what she loved and what she wanted." I refrained from saying, "and whether or not she loved me," but that's my biggest question. "Dad won't tell me anything, so I've decided to find out for myself."

"Maybe he has good reasons for not telling you. Maybe there are things you don't want to know."

"What have they told you, Paul?"

"Absolutely nothing. I get the same brush off you do if I ever ask."

"Well, I intend to find out whatever it is they don't want to tell me. I am Diana Randall's daughter. Half of my genes come from her. That should give me the right to know all there is to know about her."

"Maybe there's nothing of significance."

"If there were nothing, they wouldn't mind talking about her."

"Stay on at the newspaper. Take Steele's innocuous assignments. You can still research your own story, get a paycheck, keep your apartment, and," Paul said as he grinned and squeezed my hand, "stay where you can confide in your best friend."

I smiled, feeling the warmth of his words.

"I am your best friend, right?" he asked

"Always have been, Pablito. Always will be."

Blake, bent over papers on the old worn couch, glanced at Paul, hunched over in the only seat left, the

straight-backed office chair. Paul held the typewritten
pages on his lap, carefully stacking them beside him on
the bare concrete floor as he finished each one. Blake returned to the diary. Another big gap in time before the
next entry.

January, 1972

I stayed on at the Examiner, but also wrote
more anti-government, anti-war articles for
more liberal newspapers, and the rest of the
year fairly flew by. But I'm getting restless. I
spent Christmas at the Ranch, and though it
wasn't the same without Blake there, I didn't
want to leave. I had to work, though, so I went
back to my apartment in San Francisco.

I hear on Nixon's announcement that he'll
run for reelection, and so I'm not surprised
that he announced the withdrawal of 70,000
troops from Vietnam. I write about the 70,000
left there. Steele doesn't like it, of course. I'm
tired of my opinion articles being rejected. It's
time to do what I want for me. Find my roots.
Learn what my father won't tell me.

After making arrangements for some time
off, I asked Paul to take me to my beautiful
Rustler. I've been working too hard and not
flying enough. I walked slowly around the sleek
twin-engine, feeling blessed. Its design and
the flamboyant coloring shout speed. I run my
hand along the wing's sleek surface and stroke
a propeller in passing. The Rustler, my plane
since high school graduation, is a gift I've tak-
en for granted, but a testament to my father's

146

love. Right? I flew to LA this time last year to try to convince my dad that I have a right to know about my mother's history. I changed my mind without seeing him, though, not emotionally prepared for another brushoff. If only he'd give as freely of his voice and his time.

So, I'm off to explore my past. It feels like a life-changing step, and one I've put off too long, so when I slid into the pilot's seat. I sat still for a moment as I scanned the instrument panel and controls, remembering the first time Dad showed them to me and patiently described each one and its function. Such were the times I felt closest to Dad. He'd answer any question I had about an airplane, but turned cold and angry to any question about my mother.

It was a beautiful day, with a clear view of land and sky all the way from San Francisco to the Randall Ranch. When I flew over Marfa, I wondered what Blake was doing. My stomach clenched and my throat hurt as I thought of how easily he has forgotten me. I must do the same. I did my best to put him out of my mind. I watched for the ranch buildings to the south. I circled the place, dipping a wing when I saw Mattie in the garden, shading her eyes to look skyward. As I approached the airstrip, Mattie trotted down the path to meet me, my dog ahead of her. I jumped down, stooped to pet Shadow, whose entire body wags whenever he sees me. When I stood and opened my arms, Mattie wrapped me in her wonderful hug. God, it's good to be home.

"How long will you stay, Debbie?" she asked.

"I hope it's a long time."

"I don't know for sure. But I'll be here for a while. I'm taking a little time off from the paper to do some work of my own."

I could see Mattie waiting for more explanation, so I added, "I want to write a book, and what better place to do it than here at the ranch." That's only a partial truth, but to tell Mattie I want to research my mother's history will put her on guard to keep the secrets she's apparently sworn to keep.

After taking my horse, Trusty, for a long ride across open prairie, I returned to Harry and Mattie's humble, homey bungalow where I'd spent most of my childhood. I offered my help to put the finishing touches on supper. We had it on the kitchen table that Mattie kept covered with a worn, checkered oilcloth when Harry came in from chores. A smile creased his wind-weathered face when he saw me.

Though work worn, he's still quite handsome. Paul gets his tall, thin physique from his father. His honest brown eyes and sandy hair, too, though Harry's is thinner now. Harry shows other signs of aging...stiffness in his walk, more wrinkles around his eyes. Seeing it made me a little sad.

As we ate, I answered his and Mattie's many questions about life in the city and about Paul.

"He sends his love," I told them. "I'll try to get him to take a break and come spend some time here. It's the best possible vacation, and heaven knows Paul needs one."

There were more questions and concerns for their son's happiness, which I answered obtusely. When Harry retired to the living room to sit in his favorite chair with a magazine, I helped Mattie with the dishes. As I washed and she dried, I took a deep breath and plunged in.

"Mattie, do you have any pictures of my mother? I asked Dad if I looked like her. Of course, he wouldn't tell me."

"Deb, you know that subject is off-limits. And I don't have pictures of her. She didn't like having her picture taken. Your father must have taken her wedding pictures to Los Angeles with him. My guess is that he destroyed them."

"Why would he do that?"

"I can't answer that. I gave up understanding your father years ago."

"Was she pretty?"

"Beautiful. Beyond pretty. She looked and moved like some ethereal creature." Mattie wiped at a tear forming in the corner of her eye. "Now, not one more word about your mother. Don't ask me."

"Just tell me one thing; what was her maiden name? I don't even know that much."

Mattie put down the dishtowel and looked at me with sad eyes. "Debra, I can't. I promised Josh that I would never tell you certain things, including anything about Diana's past, so just don't ask me about her, okay?"

As I crossed the yard to the main ranch house, questions flooded my mind. As I sit here at the old writing desk in the den, I jot down a list of

questions I have to find the answers to.
Who was Diana Randall?
Where was she born?
Where did she go to school?
When did she meet Dad?
When and where did they marry?
How old was I when she died?
How did she die?
Was it my fault?
Why doesn't Dad want me to know?
Did she love him?
Did he love her?
Did she love me?

CHAPTER 24

Blake swallowed the ache in his throat that threatened to come out in a sob and looked for a diversion. "Want some coffee?" he asked Paul.

"Sure," Paul said without raising his eyes from the diary pages.

Blake filled his percolator with water, poured ground coffee from a can into the basket, and turned on the hot plate. As he sat back down and picked up his pages, Paul said, "I see why you think your brother has the cops in his pocket. But we still need to consider that he may not know where Deb is."

"Yeah. I guess." Blake handed Paul the pages he'd finished and went back to reading.

Saturday:
I got up early, invigorated by the fresh air and open spaces as I walked across the side lawn and barnyard to Mattie and Harry's house for breakfast. The sun was shining, birds singing, and the blossoms on Mattie's winter honeysuckle, kissed by raindrops from last night's shower, sparkled in the morning light. I remember helping her set out the plants to grow into a hedge at the edge of the garden when I was little. Now they're ten feet tall. They fill the air with a delicious aroma.

With a spring in my step I opened the back door and walked through the mudroom into the kitchen, just like I have almost every day of my life since I was three years old.

"Well, young lady, you're sure chipper this morning. What's up?"

"Oh nothing, Harry, just glad to be out here in the wide-open spaces. City life gets to me after a while."

"Boy, oh boy, me too. Never could understand how you and Paul can live in San Francisco."

"Your timing is great, sweetie. Hope you brought a good appetite," Mattie said.

"You can count on that. I always have a good appetite for your cooking. May I help with anything?"

"No, it's all ready. Just need to put it on the table."

Talk about comfort food! I can't think of anything more homey and comforting than breakfast at Mattie's. Homemade biscuits, sausage, gravy, and scrambled eggs reminded me I was home. When Harry left for work Mattie refilled our coffee cups and sat across the table from me.

"Sweetie, you must know how hard it is for me to refuse to tell you what you want to know about your mother. It's such a natural thing to want. I think Josh's no-talk policy is ridiculous, but I'm bound by it."

"I'm sorry, but..." I began.

Mattie held up a hand. "Believe me, it hurts me. Diana was my best friend from the time we started school in the little country schoolhouse that was halfway between our two homes. I miss her terribly. It's still hard to talk about her without tearing up."

"If you could just tell me two things, I'll quit bugging you about her."

152

Mattie wiped a tear from her eyes and asked, "What, dear? There are just certain aspects I absolutely can't talk about."

"Did she love me?"

"Oh, goodness, yes. I can answer that one. She absolutely adored you. We all did." Mattie smiled and patted Debra's hand. "What else?"

"Was it my fault she died?"

"Why, no! Absolutely not. For heaven's sake, how could it be? You weren't even two, and the brightest, best behaved, most beautiful child to ever toddle the face of the earth."

"Thanks, Mattie. That's what I needed to know." I walked around the table and hugged her. "I'll wash," I said and began clearing the table.

Taking a different tack, I asked. "How did you meet Harry, Mattie? And how did you know he was the one for you?"

"I met Harry when I was in high school in Marfa. He was a sophomore when I was a freshman. That gave me three years to get to know him pretty well. As you well know, Marfa High is a small school."

"How did you meet my dad?"

"Josh was in Harry's class and his best friend. We double-dated many times."

"You and Harry and Dad and...?"

"Oh, hardly ever the same girl twice—except Diana. He might have settled down to one steady girlfriend if Diana hadn't moved. You see, Diana's family was always moving. They left when we were sophomores, and then came back our senior year, but by then Josh and Harry had

153

gone away to college."

"Then how did he end up marrying her?"

"There you go, asking questions I'm not supposed to answer. I've already said more than your father would like."

"Sorry," I said, and after a pause, "So did you and Harry get married after you graduated high school?"

"No, I went to the same college as Josh and Harry." Mattie looked at me out of the corner of her eye. "Your mother was my college roommate. We started up our foursome then, double-dating until Josh got his aeronautics degree and moved to Los Angeles—and I quit."

"Why did you quit?"

"To marry Harry." Mattie chuckled and blushed a little. "His parents needed him on the farm. They were getting older and were not well. Harry had just graduated with a degree in agriculture and asked me to come with him. I was so much in love, I couldn't say no. We got married by a justice of the peace just before we left."

"No fancy wedding?"

"No, a very simple one. Josh and Diana stood up with us, our only witnesses."

"Oh, that's kind of sad, but I guess it doesn't take an expensive affair to make a marriage work," I mused. "Did you get any pictures?"

"No, and sometimes I regret that—and not having a wedding gown. I got married in a practical suit that has long since worn out."

"Did you regret getting married so hastily?"

"At times. When Harry's parents died, we worked our fannies off, trying to make that ranch pay the bills. Sometimes I wished we could do something besides work all the time."

"So, did Diana stay on and graduate?"

"There you go again." Mattie playfully snapped her dish towel at me. "Enough about your mother."

I let out an exasperated sigh, but forged on. "Okay, so how did you end up here?"

"Josh, who was working long hours in LA building airplanes, asked Harry to come run this ranch for him."

"Has he always owned this ranch, I mean, was it in his family?" I'm surprised I never asked that before.

"No, but it's near where he grew up. His dad and mom never owned land, just share-cropped. I think he always hated that and wanted to buy land of his own as soon as he could afford it."

"When did he buy this place?"

"It was after your mother graduated. I guess I can tell you she finished college in LA, but hated city living, so Josh bought this ranch for her. She loved this part of Texas more than any other place her parents had lived. Josh couldn't run it though. He was building a business in California.

"So, that's when you moved here?"

"No, we couldn't. We were still taking care of Harry's parents. They were both in bad health. I had Paulie by then, and Harry was determined to make a go of the family ranch, so he refused."

"That must have been before I was born?" I squeezed out the dishcloth and wiped gravy spills from the electric stove top that replaced the wood-burning range they had when I was growing up.

"Yes. He asked us again the next year. We'd just buried Harry's parents, and Paulie was learning to walk. Harry loved the ranch on the Pecos where he grew up, and with rain, the prospects were promising. He said no, again. But nature was against us. We managed to hang on a few more years until a drought and then a plague of locusts wiped us out. Paulie was five when Harry finally accepted Josh's offer and became foreman of the Randall Ranch. I wasn't happy about it, but I didn't have a choice."

"You didn't want to come?" I was surprised.

"I was angry at Josh. Diana was gone by then. If Harry had been willing to move when she was still alive, I'd have jumped at the chance. I thought I could help her."

"Help her? With what?"

"Oh, honey, you keep getting me to say things I'm not supposed to talk about. I'll just say that when Harry finally wanted to come here, I didn't. I thought it would be too hard to live here without her." Mattie smiled wryly as she folded her dishtowel over the towel rack next to the sink.

"What about me?"

"You were my salvation. Just three years old and in need of a mother. You gave me purpose. You and Paulie. That's all I lived for."

"Are you sorry you came?"

"No, not at all. I came to love this place. It's home. Harry and I are happy here, though I have to admit there were some rough times in those early years. Harry was more devoted to Josh than to me, it seemed. I was jealous."

"So, who took care of me before you came? You said I was only two when my mother died, but I was three when you came here," I asked turning back to rinse out the sink.

"You had nannies and a string of housekeepers from the time you were born. Josh thought Diana should have help with an infant, so he hired women to keep up the mansion he built for her and to look after you. That doesn't mean she didn't love you. She did. She was involved in your care, but having a nanny gave her time to pursue other interests."

"What interests?"

"She was an artist, far more talented than she knew. She loved painting and writing—mostly poetry—but, to her, those were just hobbies," Mattie took the dishcloth from me and wiped the table. "She was always involved in some cause or another, always wanting to make life better for everyone." She turned to me with a look of horror. "Look what you made me do. Your father would have my hide."

"Just one more question, Mattie," I begged. "Did Dad hate her? Is that why he refuses to talk about her?"

"No, not at all. His love for Diana bordered on hero worship. I don't believe he ever stopped loving her, but his love was too possessive, too protective." Mattie shook her head at me. "I've said more than I should, so remember, that's just my opinion."

"But why? If he loved her, you'd think..."

"Your father has always been a man's man. Probably how he was raised. Men brought up in those days were taught not to cry. Still are, actually. Showing such emotion was considered a sign of weakness. Early on, when I tried to get him to talk about her, he'd choke up and fight back tears. But all he said was, 'Enough, Mattie. What's done is behind us. Talking won't bring her back, and then he'd stomp out, get on his horse, and ride away. That's how he dealt with emotion. Riding a horse at breakneck speed or flying off in one of his airplanes."

The next page was written in Debra's perfect cursive in blue ink, some of it blotched as if the ink had puddled from a fountain pen or water had dropped on it. He read:

Monday:

I'm sitting on the back veranda staring at the river and feeling glum. Maybe recording my really horrible terrible day will make me feel better. To start the day, I decided the Marfa High School might be the place to begin looking, so I drove the ranch pickup. I chose the long drive over flying in order to avoid seeing Blake. It would be awkward to land at his airport when we aren't speaking to each other. I parked in front of my old high school and went in. I studied the framed class photos that lined the hallway walls. I found Mattie's picture, Matilda Mae Morgan, it said.

I've never given a lot of thought to Mattie's looks. She was just Mattie, my substitute—and wonderful—mother. But seeing her at age 17 or 18, even in a black and white head shot, causes me to compare the Mattie I know with this very pretty girl. Dark curls frame her oval face with her slightly turned up nose and bright smile. She reminds me a little of Sally Fields in the movie The Flying Nun. And she hasn't changed all that much, once I think about it. Some gray streaks in her dark brown hair and a few extra pounds, but really, it's her smile and her expressive brown eyes that make Mattie beautiful.

I looked for a Diana in the same class. There were two. I had no trouble guessing which one was my mother. The picture of Diana Dupris looked so familiar it took my breath away, although that hardly makes sense. I guess it's because I resemble her. My gosh! She was beautiful.

I found Josh Randall and Harry Diamond's pictures in the frame next to Mattie's class, both nice-looking boys. Seeing Harry at that age was like looking at Paul.

I went to the office and asked the secretary, "Is it possible to buy a copy of the school annual for 1943?"

"I'll have to look in our archives." The woman, new since I graduated, seemed pleased to have a diversion. I followed her down the hall.

"You're in luck. We have two. One original that we'll want to keep and one that was turned back to us after the owner passed away. I'll give that one to you, if you like."

I thanked her and paged through it looking for my mother's senior picture. It's there, a two-inch high, black and white head shot. I thumb through the back pages, hoping to see Diana or Mattie in the snapshots. I find one. The Marfa Swim team. There are five girls and two boys lined up on the edge of a swimming pool. Mattie and Diana stand side by side in the middle. Mattie is almost a head shorter than Diana and heavier. Not fat, at all but with a fuller figure. Diana is willowy, and her hair is almost white in the black and white picture. She must have been a platinum blond. I notice that she and Mattie have hooked their little fingers together. Staring at it, I can just feel their friendship, their reliance on each other, or maybe it's more that Diana gets her strength from Mattie, who is smiling broadly, while Diana looks down, hiding her face from the camera.

Next, I went to the newspaper office and searched their archived copies on microfiche for every mention of Diana Dupris. The first I found has a picture with it. It's shows a delicate, fairy-like, ten-year-old girl at a baby grand piano. "Diana Dupris Wows the Audience at Mrs. Gray's Piano Recital."

The next article is about the Marfa High School annual play. The headline reads: "The Marfa High School Presents an Adaptation of Gone with the Wind." The article says there will be performances Friday evening, Saturday afternoon, and Saturday night. "The lovely senior, Diana Dupris, will play Scarlett O'Hara." I wish they'd printed her picture.

"We will be closing in twenty minutes," the receptionist interrupted. "You're welcome to come back tomorrow. Or I can make copies for you if you know what you want."

"If you can make copies, that would be perfect, would you please?" I gave her dates and page numbers of the newspapers I'd found that mentioned Diana Dupris, thinking I could read them in the privacy of the ranch house. When she handed the copies to me, I thanked her and walked into the cool of the early evening.

I hadn't eaten since breakfast and decided to get a bite at the café across the street before driving back to the ranch. Seated at a table next to the window with a menu in my hand, I heard a voice that almost gave me a heart attack.

Although his back was to me, I recognized my former boyfriend immediately. I froze, unable to take a breath. The lovely brunette with big dark eyes and bright red lips seemed to hang on his every word. His voice was too soft for me to make out

160

the words, but they must have been endearing. The woman reached across the table and touched a hand so familiar, I felt violated.

I grabbed my bag and tiptoed toward the door. "Sorry, I've changed my mind," I whispered to the astonished waitress. "Here. A little tip for your time. I put a five-dollar bill in her hand, and with a quick glance at the couple at the table, I slipped out the door, relieved that Blake didn't see me.

All the way home, thoughts tumbled in my head. Feelings that I can't justify bubbled in my chest and stomach—and still do. I feel betrayed, insulted, and, most of all, heartbroken. I thought I'd gotten over him. Obviously, I haven't.

"Get a damned grip, Debra!" He must not be the man for me. If he can forget me so much easier than I can forget him, he must not have really loved me. What makes me so hard to love? I'd like to know. Oops. Tears are dripping onto the paper as I write this. All the way home, it was hard to see the road because of the darned tears. I've got to quit this, so to hell with him.

How long have I sat here, crying? The sun's edging to the horizon. The mansion seems bigger and lonelier than ever, and writing this doesn't make me feel any better. I think I'll go turn Trusty out and go back to San Francisco in the morning. I don't know when I'll be back—if ever!

Blake drew in a quick gasp of air. Was this a clue to her disappearance. Was she so depressed she'd think of suicide? No. Not Debra. She just couldn't. Wouldn't. Would she?

"What?" Paul asked. "Did you find something?"

"I don't know. Don't think so. Just got to a place where she sounds depressed. You'll see it. It's probably nothing." Blake resumed reading. The next page was typewritten.

(Early Tuesday morning)

After turning my horse into the pasture, I came back in the house, cut the photo of Diana Dupris from the yearbook and framed the black-and-white image as I stared at her wide eyes that seemed to be begging something.

"Mother, why did you leave me? I aim to find out, if it's the last thing I do."

I coaxed Shadow up on the bed, put my arm around him, and succumbed to the "feeling" that had threatened to overwhelm me since I left Marfa. It was still dark when I woke and took some aspirin. When I went back to sleep, I had strange erotic dreams of a man whose face kept changing. One minute it looked like Paul; the next, it was Blake, and then it was the face of a mannequin, a plastic shape with no eyes or mouth.

I'll leave right after breakfast, taking my mother's photo, the yearbook, and the printouts from the newspaper in an empty briefcase from my father's office.

That's it? Blake frantically looked for another page. There was no more. If she'd decided to kill herself, she'd have left a note here, surely. What had she found in the newspapers? Could they hold a secret to her disappearance? Paul interrupted his thoughts.

"Blake, there's one thing I keep coming back to. Listen to this: 'I clutched the prism as if it were a lifeline as the sound of water crescendoed in my head and a voice like an angel called my name.' I wish I knew more about that prism."

"Yeah, I've seen her grab that thing. She was holding on to it just before she told me to get out of her car the first time we broke up. She was pale and looked terrified." Blake paused and frowned at Paul. "Tell me what you know about it."

"I was with her when she got it and have seen her wear it almost constantly ever since, but I never have understood the intrigue. It seems like it was somehow associated with her spells."

"So, what are you thinking? The prism brought on a spell that caused her to lose her mind?" Blake couldn't forget how crazy she seemed after the Christmas party. How much had the prism affected that?

"Maybe the prism's the key. Want to fly me to the Ranch? Mom might have some answers."

"I guess I can put off murdering my brother a little longer," Blake said, wryly, "if there's a chance something else happened to her. Besides, I want to do some of my own research here in Marfa. See if I can find out what was in the newspapers she brought back to California to read. That could also be a clue." Blake handed the last pages of the manuscript to Paul.

CHAPTER 25

Blake dropped Paul at the ranch, flew back to Marfa, and dug through the same archives Debra had seen. Anything related to Dupris and Randall. In the meantime, Paul sat down with Mattie.

"Mom, you've always been careful about what to say to me about Deb's mother, but I'm not a kid anymore and Debra's gone, so I hope you'll answer some questions for me."

"Okay, sure. I'll tell you what I can, though I can't imagine how it could help find her."

"Maybe it won't, but at least it will let me know more about her, maybe more than she ever knew about herself—and should have."

"Now, don't get judgmental, Paul. I was following her father's orders, and he was doing what he thought best for her. And maybe it was." Mattie folded the dishtowel and sat at the table across from her son. "Now, what is it you want to know?"

"How did her mother die? Did she have some kind of, uh, spells? And do you know anything about where Deb's prism came from?" Paul asked. "I know her father gave it to her for her tenth birthday. I was there. But I can't figure out what was so special about it. He gave her a lot of jewelry, all more valuable than that thing." Paul nervously rattled off questions as they came to mind. Mattie chose to answer the last one.

"That thing is right. I thought she was better off without it, so I hid it in a desk drawer in the office in the hangar when she was four." Mattie frowned and shook her head. "Debbie cried when she couldn't find it at bedtime, but she soon got over it and forgot about it altogether."

"You mean she had it before her father gave it to her?" Paul didn't think his mother was making sense.

"Yes. Josh obviously found it in the desk that day he gave it to her and pocketed it. It was her birthday, and either he didn't know what it was or where it came from, or he felt forced to give her something and that was all he had. He had arrived without a present for her, and you know he always brought her a gift. She expected it, whether it was her birthday or not. He had to give her something so he pulled that trinket out of his pocket and pretended he'd planned to surprise her with it all along. He felt pretty lucky when it proved to be such a hit with her."

"Why did you take it away from her when she was four?"

"When we came here, Deb was three, a poor little waif without a mother and with a father who was almost never home. He hired housekeepers and nannies for her, but she needed permanence. That's when I knew I'd stay here and take care of her as long as she called this place home. At the time we arrived, Debra was suffering abandonment issues even though she had all the attention and material things money could buy.

"The housekeeper who had been caring for her told me Debra had to have her prism before she would take a nap or go to sleep at bedtime. She said, 'If you can't get Debbie to go to sleep, let her have her bauble.' At first, I thought she said, bottle, but she meant the pendant. She was using it like a pacifier. Deb would scream and cry until she got it. I took it off the chain, afraid she'd strangle herself. Then she'd hold it, stare at it, and watch the rainbows until she fell asleep. But she'd wake up crying that her head hurt. She often had nightmares as well. I gave her the pendant until one night I couldn't find it and was forced to find another way to settle her down and get her to sleep. I held her and read her stories and sang to her. I finally rocked her to sleep. She slept through the night, had no nightmares, woke up smiling, with no headache. When I found the thing, I hid it and changed her bedtime ritual. We always had stories, singing, and rocking. Her headaches went away."

"Until she was ten," Paul said.

"Yes, I guess so. They did come back after that, didn't they? I hardly noticed, though, because she seldom told me."

"Where did the prism come from in the first place?"

"It belonged to Debra's mother. She got it before Debbie was born. Let me back up a bit. I'll tell you everything I know, whether Josh likes it or not, if you think it will help find her. Diana finished college at UCLA to be close to Josh, but she hated California. She'd grown up in the country and felt hemmed in. She started volunteering for worthy causes that overwhelmed her. According to Josh, she was always worn out and crying about some homeless person, or neglected animal, or even stories about people in other countries facing starvation or persecution of some kind."

"What about the prism?"

"Hush. Don't hurry me. I'm getting to that. You wanted to know everything, right?"

"Yes. Please go on."

"So, Josh bought this ranch and had the biggest, nicest house he could imagine built for her. She might have been happier if he hadn't hired help for her. She always thought they were his spies to keep her in line. Even here on the ranch, she managed to find and bring home strays. She took in every animal, sometimes injured wild ones besides dogs and cats that people dumped on the road. Josh finally put his foot down and said absolutely no more."

"I can imagine Josh saying that," Paul said. "He's always given Debra everything she asked for, but he wouldn't even let her have a dog or a cat in their apartment in LA."

Mattie nodded. "Well, Diana couldn't take it. Not long after their wedding, she told Josh she was leaving him, and she did."

"She left him? When?"

"She heard about a spiritual retreat in Colorado that sounded like just what she needed. She sent me a brochure and asked me to go with her. She said it embraced everything she and I believed in. According to the brochure, it taught people to find their true calling and to connect with spiritual ancestors who could guide them through life. It sounded hokey to me, and I told her I wouldn't go. I had a toddler to take care of."

"Is that where she got the prism?"

"Yes, it's their trademark. So, Diana came home with the prism and religion. She adopted their doctrine wholeheartedly and said she'd do whatever her spiritual guides told her to do. One was to forgive her husband and reconcile with him. I always suspected the people who ran the organization knew she'd never be able to support herself and talked her into staying with Josh, because he had the money."

"Josh paid for this retreat?" Paul asked.

"Well, I assume so. She had no income of her own." Mattie's voice held contempt. "I know he begged her not to divorce him."

"Sounds like he loved her."

Mattie shrugged. "Yes. He always loved her in his way. Worshiped her is more like it. But he had no idea how to show his love. Josh thinks money is the answer to everything."

Paul frowned. "Go on—about the prism."

"I came to visit her for a week after she returned. She wore that thing all the time, and sometimes while she was holding it, she'd seem to go into a sort of trance. She was communicating with her ancestors, or some such hogwash. She was pregnant." Mattie looked thoughtful. "I thought maybe it was the pregnancy that made her seem so distant. She was never comfortable with it, sure it made her unattractive."

"What kind of a place was this spiritual retreat?"

"I don't know a lot about it. I read the brochure once, but I threw it away because it sounded like a bunch of hooey to me. She was deeply into it, though. She said they had group sessions where everyone talked about their past lives."

"What do you mean?"

"Well, at first I thought she just meant they talked about childhood memories and trauma. She said there was that, too, but also a regression into her past, through her ancestors. Everyone staying there had prisms exactly alike, and in their individual sessions, they'd say some kind of mantra and invite their grandparents and other ancestors further back to tell her things she needed to know about her life. She said she learned that she had lived before, centuries before, and that she was her own great-great-grandmother."

"Weird."

"I know. I told you it was balderdash. But it made her seem more fragile than ever."

Mattie stared into the distance, remembering, "Once, I asked her why she seemed so sad, and she said I'd be sad too, if I'd been through the hardships and had seen all the horrors she had seen."

"So maybe this prism somehow caused both Diana's death and Debra's disappearance."

Mattie harrumphed. "Don't be silly. There is no magic in that cheap chunk of glass. However, I think the mumbo-jumbo they put into her head, coupled with the way Josh treated her, may have led to the accident."

"How did Josh treat her?"

"He was overprotective, authoritarian. He doted on her, gave her everything she asked for, but he wouldn't let her have a single idea of her own. He wanted to control her every move, thinking he knew what was good for her better than she did. She had no freedom. When she came back from Colorado, it was worse, especially after Deb was born. He demanded that she account for every minute of her time and for every penny she spent. I guess he was afraid she'd escape again. And with the nanny to take care of Deb, she was convinced Josh didn't trust her to care for her own child."

"What was it she wanted that he wouldn't let her have?"

"Well, I can see his point on that," Mattie said. "If she'd had her way, she'd have turned this place into a shelter for every animal or person who didn't have a home or was being mistreated. She'd have given away every cent he could make for every charity she heard of."

"Looks like there could have been a compromise somewhere between the two extremes."

"I'm not sure either one of them could have found a middle ground that would have pleased them. Diana was trying to save the world. When she couldn't do that, she was unable to save herself."

"Where is this place in Colorado? Do you know the name of it?"

"No. I don't remember what it was called. I think it was in Denver. Might have been Colorado Springs, or maybe Boulder. I think the word 'prism' was in the name, somehow. Or maybe it was pyramid. She always said it was the power of the pyramid that took her back to her beginnings."

Paul picked up the phone to call Marfa. Blake had just walked into his office, armed with newspapers when the phone rang. "How soon can you pick me up? We're going to Colorado."

As Blake flew, Paul read the printouts from the newspaper to him.

The first page he picked up was a page of wedding announcements with grainy pictures of couples with last names under them. He scanned the page until he saw, "Dupris — Randall" Even in the black-and-white imperfect photo, they were a handsome couple.

"Wow," Paul said. "Deb's mom was beautiful. Deb

looks a lot like her." He read the short announcement: "Diana Dupris and Joshua Randall were united in marriage on October 25, 1947, in the Presidio County Courthouse."

He looked at the next page and found a birth announcement. "To Diana and Josh Randall, a girl, 7 lbs, 6 oz. April 8, 1948." He quickly did the math and said, "She obviously wasn't premature with that birth weight. Debra would have noticed she was an accident and probably wondered if her parents actually wanted her."

Next, Paul read the obituary. "Diana Randall, age 26, died March 14, 1950. She is survived by her husband, Joshua T. Randall and a daughter, Debra. Her parents, Susan and Donald Dupris, and a brother, James Dupris preceded her in death."

He looked at the next paper, dated a day later.

"Diana Randall died in a tragic accident on the Randall Ranch in western Presidio County last Tuesday. Police investigated the death and ruled out foul play. According to her husband, Josh Randall, and Esther Alton, a housekeeper, Diana was alone when she fell into the Rio Grande River near their house. She was unable to swim."

"Does that sound suspicious to you?" Blake asked. "With the police looking into it?"

"If I remember right, Mom told me once that she was on a swim team in high school. I remember her saying that Deb's mother was a better swimmer than she was."

"That could have upset, Debra, if she knew that."

The men rode in silence the rest of the way to Denver.

CHAPTER 26

Sergeant Louis Stanton, deputy sheriff for Boulder County, yawned and reached for his coffee cup as another boring staff meeting got off to a slow start. He slowly sipped the strong brew as the sheriff intoned his pep talk before assigning the duties of the day.

A knock on the door preceded the secretary's entrance. She blurted, "I'm sorry to interrupt, but these gentlemen insist it's urgent. They said they had to catch you while everyone's together. The PD sent them here."

A tall, thin man about the same age as Louis entered the room. Unlike Louis, his sandy hair hung below his shoulders, he looked like he hadn't shaved for a few days, and he wore jeans and cowboy boots. His floral shirt was untucked and wrinkled. He strode in and slapped a photo on the table in front of the sheriff. "Have any of you seen this person? I have reason to believe she might be in the Boulder area."

Behind him stood a shorter, stockier guy with dark hair and blue eyes who looked at least as disheveled as the first.

The sheriff studied the photo for half a second and shook his head. "Nope," he said, passing it to the deputy on his right.

That deputy picked it up and held it to the light. He let out a low whistle and said, "No, I'd sure remember her if I had. Is she a movie star?"

The hippie cowboy didn't answer. When the picture came to Louis, he stared, stunned, his heart racing.

Damn. Was he destined to be haunted by this lady for the rest of his life? He looked up and nodded. "Yes. I've seen her. Who is she?"

"She is the missing daughter of the richest man in California. Perhaps you've heard of Randall Aircraft?"

"I'll be damned!" the sheriff exclaimed. "I heard they finally closed the case on her. But that was in California, so it never crossed my mind that she could be here." He looked at Louis. "You've seen her? Are you sure it was her?"

"Quite sure, sir."

"Do you know where she is?" the first young man asked, his voice squeaky with hope and fear.

"No. I have no idea."

"Stanton, go with these boys. Your name, sir?"

"Paul Diamond, and this is Blake Mallory."

"Okay, Stanton, see what you can do to help Mr. Diamond and Mr. Mallory find the lady."

"Can we get out of here?" Diamond asked as Louis led him to his cubicle. "Let's find a quiet coffee shop."

When the three were seated and had ordered coffee, Paul asked, "When did you see her? Was she all right? And why the hell didn't you tell anyone?"

"Hold on," Louis said, raising his hand from the table. "What was I supposed to tell? I didn't know she was anyone but who she said she was, which at the time didn't mean a thing to me. Not until the real Tiffany Adams came looking for her car."

"She told you her name was Tiffany Adams?" Paul couldn't think of any reason Debra would do that, and his hopes plummeted. Whomever this guy had seen, it must have been someone else, someone who looked a lot like Deb. He felt like crying.

"Well, I guess she didn't really tell me as much as I told her. But she sure as hell didn't deny it."

"Was she wearing a pendant around her neck?" Blake asked.

"Yes, a piece of cut glass on a gold chain. She seemed quite attached to it."

Paul's hopes soared again. "Maybe you should tell the story from the beginning."

Louis nodded. "It was the night of the flood."

"The flood?"

"Yes, we had a doozy around the end of May. Heavy rains in the mountains. Flooded some of the mountain towns and the lower lying areas of Boulder, too. I'd been called to investigate a domestic-violence call in James-town, and as I was driving back, I came up on a new, bright yellow Camaro barely pulled off at the edge of the narrow highway. It was pouring rain, but I had to get out and investigate.

"I shined a light in the passenger side window and saw a woman slumped over in the seat. I tried the door, but it was locked, so I kept tapping on the window. I was about to break it when she stirred. She really looked out of it, but I finally got her to unlock the door. I was sure she was drunk or stoned or both."

"Not if it was Debra," Paul said.

Louis shrugged. "Well, I'd have sworn she was by her behavior, but you're right. When I finally got her to the hospital, she tested completely drug and alcohol free."

"You took her to the hospital instead of booking her? She must have been..." Blake said.

"Wait there's more, much more," Louis interrupted. "I walked her to my vehicle and handcuffed her to the grab bar while I went back to look for ID. There was no purse, or container of any kind that I could find. The registration listed the owner of the car as Tiffany Adams."

Paul and Blake looked at each other, neither able to imagine Debra as a car thief.

"I started down the canyon, but ran into a mudslide blocking the road. Turned around to go back to Jamestown, and found a bridge washed out and the road flooded. Like I said it was a bad storm—a big enough flash flood to destroy the bridge in that short length of time. We'd have been trapped on a road where we were likely to be washed down the canyon, except that I knew about a forest-service cabin up the side of the mountain. It's about a mile climb."

Louis shook his head. "She got pretty feisty when she got out in the rain, though looking back on it, I wasn't much of a gentleman. I called her a dopehead and accused her of drunk driving. She kept demanding her rights, saying she hadn't done anything wrong. She did convince me to take off her handcuffs that I'd hooked to the grab bar when she pointed out that she'd rather be free to jump if the Bronco started to slide off the road and down the mountain. I'm embarrassed that she had to remind me of that."

"Does kind of sound like Deb," Paul said.

"When we got to the trail head, I handed her a backpack from the back of the Bronco. I carried the flashlight and another bag and yelled, 'Follow me.' Then I took off up the path. She had to run to keep up with me, but I figured it would do her good, maybe run off some of the booze. I kept going until I heard her yell, 'Wait,' and looked back. She was sitting against the trunk of a large tree.

"I turned around and yelled at her to get away from that tree. With the lightning as close as it was, it could fall on top of her.'

"She said, 'I can't go on. I don't think I can take another step.' She didn't look like she could, either. She seemed completely exhausted. But we weren't out of the floodplain yet. We had to go on, so I helped her up and pushed her up the hill in front of me.

"The cabin was dark, dank, and cold, but at least it wasn't raining inside. She just stood right where I let go of her and watched me move around the cabin looking for a lantern and some matches. When I got some light in the place, she slumped onto a wooden chair at the table while I built a fire in a pot-bellied stove. I noticed a towel on a hook and tossed that to her. By then I was afraid she was close to hypothermia. I told her to get out of her wet clothes before she caught pneumonia. Her teeth were chattering."

Blake groaned. Paul said, "My God, poor Deb."

Louis frowned. "I know. I was worried and doing the best I could. I got her a blanket and told her to wrap in it. She was worried about me seeing her naked, so I started to step out in the rain. But she said. "You don't have to go out in the storm. Just turn your back. So, I did and tended the fire while I was at it. Got it roaring and pushed the only bed, an army cot, close to the stove.

"Once she was wrapped up, sitting on the cot, I wrapped more blankets around her. She finally stopped shivering and lay down. When she was asleep, I hung her clothes behind the stove. I undressed in the corner and found a sleeping bag. Laid my clothes out to dry, too. Curled up on the other side of the stove and went to sleep with rain still pounding the roof of the cabin."

Louis paused, and Blake said, "Go on."

Nodding, Louis continued. "I questioned her the next day, but she wouldn't tell me anything. I called her Tiffany. She asked how I knew that was her name. But she never denied that it was.

"It quit raining, and I kept going down the hill to check on the road. Finally, after two days, they got the mudslide cleared enough for us to get out. But on the way down the trail, it started raining hard again, and a little stream had washed out the path. I don't know if she tripped and fell into it, or if she passed out, but I heard her fall and turned around. She was unconscious face down in the water.

"Oh, God, no!" both men gasped in unison.

"No, she was okay, last I knew. I carried her down to the Bronco and took her directly to the hospital. I radioed ahead so they had a gurney waiting. She didn't wake up until they had her on a bed in a cubicle in the ER. I was worried, so I stayed while they checked her out. Like I said, her blood tested clean. When she had revived completely and lab tests, scans, and her vital signs indicated she was okay, they released her. She had no belongings, just the clothes she was wearing. Jeans, cowboy boots, and a cotton shirt."

"Where'd she go?"

"I have no idea. I never saw her again. But the real Tiffany Adams came looking for her car. She had loaned it to a girl she didn't know, and stayed in Jamestown to ride back with her boyfriend. When I asked her the young woman's name, she said she never thought to ask."

"So, you can't help us find her?"

"I thought if you could tell me more about her... or that maybe something I told you could..." Louis looked down. "Oh, hell, I'm sorry. I guess I've been no help at all."

"Can you tell us more about what she was like in the hospital? Did she seem confused at all?" Paul asked.

Louis thought for a moment. "Well, yeah, she seemed pretty disoriented, at first at least. But that's what one would expect just waking up in a strange place."

"Tells us what she said."

"Well she wasn't very cooperative. Wouldn't answer questions. I remember the nurse saying, 'No, Tiffany. Please look at me.' I'd told them her name was Tiffany Adams. The nurse kept pleading, 'I'm here to help you, but I can hardly do that unless you talk to me.'

"She, uh, Debra, didn't want to open her eyes and when she did, it seemed hard for her to focus.

"The nurse asked if she hurt anywhere and she nodded.

"When the nurse asked where, she said, 'My head; I have a gargantuan headache,' and asked for aspirin. But the nurse wouldn't give her anything without the doctor ordering it. The nurse quizzed her about allergies to medication, and Debra just shrugged like she didn't know. When the nurse asked if she had frequent fainting spells, she said, 'I fainted?'

"She didn't remember fainting or falling. The nurse asked what was the last thing she remembered. She didn't answer, so the nurse explained what she knew—

what I'd told her—and asked, 'Does any of that ring a bell?'

"Again, Debra didn't say anything, just looked at me. I was standing near the foot of the bed she was lying on. She looked confused, like she wondered who I was. They asked if she had epilepsy. She just shook her head a tiny bit, and winced, closing her eyes, like it hurt.

"The doctor ordered an x-ray and an EEG to see if this was the result of a seizure or a head injury, and I just stayed until they took her to x-ray. I watched her sign her name, and it looked like a struggle for her. They had to keep urging her. She finally scrawled, 'Tiffany Adams' but it seemed difficult for her. The name was printed at the top of the form. I signed as a witness. They asked for her belongings, and that's when I noticed she had a really expensive watch besides that pendant. Nothing else. I left then, but I called back later to find out the results. They said everything looked good, and she was feeling much better, so they let her go home."

After hearing the whole story, as Louis knew it, Paul's heart sank again. Apparently, Debra's spells—and memory loss—had become a lot worse. Maybe that's why she left. They were out of control, and she didn't want anyone to know. Was it possible it could get so bad she would kill herself? Is that what her mother had done?

"What made you think she was in Boulder?" Louis asked.

"I was grasping at straws, really, but I found out a bit about the history of that prism. It belonged to her mother. She died when Debra was a toddler. The way Deb treasured it and the spells and headaches she got sometimes when she held it made me think it might have something to do with her disappearance. I found out it came from a spiritual church or organization of some kind in Colorado. In Denver, I found an organization with the initials P.R.I.S.M. No one had seen or heard of her there, but they told me there were two more branches, one in Boulder and one in Colorado Springs. I came here first because it's closer. Do you know of anything like that? We couldn't find a listing for it. It's a long shot, but she might have contacted them, if they're still open."

CHAPTER 27

Three men approached the address on a Boulder, Colorado, side street. There was no mistaking the place with the prisms. A large, ornately carved, dark mahogany door with a window was recessed in the middle of a building with a stone façade. The window was mostly stained glass of myriad colors and shapes, but in the middle, framed in wood, was a square of clear glass on which gold lettering spelled:

P.R.I.S.M.
Pyramidal Studies

Prismatic Restoration of
Intergenerational Spiritual Memory

Beneath the frame, as part of the stained glass, was an exact image of the prism they'd all seen Debra clutch tightly.

Louis knocked, waited, knocked again, and tried the door. Locked. Hanging on the doorknob was a sign.
Classes in Progress, Do Not Disturb.
It gave a phone number to call for information. Louis knocked on the door again, harder, and repeatedly.

Inside, the director, Rachelle, jumped. No one ever knocked, or in this case, pounded on the door during a session. The sign on the doorknob was usually enough to discourage people. She was in the middle of a crisis.

One of her charges was missing from the infirmary. She decided to ignore the rude visitor, whoever it was.

But, as the knocker persisted, rapping louder and more insistently, Rachelle veered to the door and peered through the window. Three men, one in uniform, stood waiting, but not patiently. As the uniformed officer raised his hand to knock again, she pulled a key from her pocket and opened the door.

"Excuse me for not answering sooner, but as you see," she pointed to the sign, "we are in session and prefer to be contacted by phone."

The uniformed man was a sheriff, and he showed her a badge. "We won't take much of your time."

"Well, all right. Come in and have a seat."

Wow, Paul thought, as he stared at the petite, heavily made up, dark-haired woman wearing a flowing, bright floral caftan, belted at the waist with a gold, tasseled cord. *What kind of place is this?*

To the sound of soft flute music, Paul, Blake, and Louis followed the woman through a dimly lit foyer. The fragrance of incense was overpowering. As their eyes adjusted, they took in the deep maroon and cobalt colors in the geometric patterned rug, repeated in the plush upholstered chairs. Dark tapestry covered the walls, and several candles on a single mahogany table furnished the only light—except for the dancing rainbows from light refracted through the front door window.

Without waiting to be seated, Louis said, "We are looking for Debra Randall. Here is a picture of her."

Paul held out the photo. "Have you seen her?"

Rachelle visibly flinched and then seemed to measure her words. "She is here as part of this program, but please believe me, I didn't know her identity until just a few minutes ago."

"Would you explain that, please?" asked the officer.

Blake, didn't wait. He refused to sit. "Where is she?" he demanded. "I want to see her. Now."

"Well, I just..."

"Excuse me," A woman interrupted, bursting through a curtain of colored beads. "I checked the bedroom and the baths. She isn't there. I checked with Duane on my way back. He hasn't seen her, either."

"Debra!" Paul yelped.

Rachelle gulped, nodded slightly, and addressed the messenger. "Did you check the roof, Candy?"

"No, not yet. I will."

"I will, too," Paul said. He followed Blake, who was already on Candy's heels, almost running, urging her to hurry.

"Sirs," Rachelle yelled to stop them. "You can't..."

Louis put his hand on her arm. "How easy would it be to jump off the roof? And how long has she been gone?"

"You think she's in danger of harming herself?" Rachelle asked in alarm.

"I hope not, but apparently those young men, who know her better than I do, think so. Will you take me there?"

As Louis followed Rachelle up the stairs, he asked, "Have you called her father since you found out who she is?"

"No, there hasn't been time."

To Blake's immense relief, Debra was lying on a chaise lounge, sleeping, a smile indicating a pleasant dream.

He held back, and Paul reached her first.

Dropping to his knees, Paul stroked her arm. "Kitten. Are you okay? Debra, it's me. Paul."

Her eyes fluttered open.

"Pablito. You found me." Her arms entwined his neck as she pulled him close, kissing his cheeks. Tasting his tears.

"Here. Let me sit up," she said. "I have to make sure I'm not dreaming."

"You're not dreaming, Kitten, unless I'm dreaming, too. And if I am, I don't ever want to wake up.

"Debra," Blake's voice was choked and tears filled his eyes, making them gleam like the deepest blue sapphire.

"Blake? You came with Paul? I was afraid I'd never see you again." Tears filled her emerald eyes, and she reached for him with both arms.

In an instant he was holding her in a tender embrace, kissing her forehead, hair, cheeks, and finally her lips.

With her arms still around Blake's neck, she asked, "How did you guys find me? I only just found myself."

Louis stood looking on with a bemused smile. When Debra noticed him, she asked, "You look so familiar. Do I know you?"

"You may not remember. I used to call you Tiffany."

A slow dawning crossed Debra's beautiful face. "On the mountain, in a storm. I think you saved my life. Thank you."

Anxious to leave, Debra, clad only in the toga furnished by the P.R.I.S.M. foundation, asked Rachelle for her clothes.

"You want to leave? But the session isn't over. We discourage people from leaving early."

"Really?" Louis asked, frowning. "You're trying to prevent her leaving after all she's been through?"

"Well, no, of course not," Rachelle rushed to say, blushing. "But, Debra, you've paid in full. We do not refund..."

"Keep the watch," Debra said, referring to the diamond-studded Rolex she'd given them as collateral. "Now that I know who I am, I have things to take care of. I'm out of here." She pulled on her jeans, socks and boots, and turned her back to pull off the toga and replace it with her shirt.

Debra and the three men walked to a quiet café at the end of the block for a bite to eat and to catch up on months of history. Debra had stories to tell, and none of the three men wanted to wait another minute to hear them.

"But first we must call Josh and my mom," Paul said as he motioned her into a booth next to a window and slid in across from her.

"Call Mattie, if you wish, but swear her to secrecy. I want to surprise Dad in person. I have a lot of questions for him, and this time he'll have to answer."

"I was sure that Kent had kidnapped you, but instead, you chose to come here. Why?" Blake asked, sliding in beside her. "Does that prism have some kind of power over you?"

Debra looked down and fingered the prism. "No, but it helped me regain my memory, I think. And Kent did capture me. I left my apartment in a rage, throwing caution to wind, as I focused on forcing Dad to explain some things. And..." Debra faltered as tears sprang to her eyes.

"I walked right into Kent's arms. He was waiting for me, next to my car."

Looking into Blake's eyes, she continued. "I was terrified when I saw him. I'd been so upset about what I'd found in my research that I never once thought about Kent until he stepped in front of me." Wiping away a tear with her thumb, she continued. "All I could think was that I couldn't let him see how scared I was. No matter what he did, I must not give him the satisfaction of showing fear. I didn't want to give him that power over me." Debra took a deep, shuddering breath and continued, "But I thought I would die. Maybe not right away. I knew he wanted to torture me first. I thought that maybe if I fought hard enough, he'd kill me sooner. I'd kill myself before I became his sex slave."

With tears running down his cheeks unchecked, Blake said, "I'm so sorry, Deb. I should have killed him a long time ago."

"Goddammit!" Paul yelped. "If I'd known..."

"Shut up, Paul," Blake interrupted, his icy, cobalt eyes flashing a warning that Paul heeded.

"Please go on, Deb," Blake said, "if it's not too painful."

Debra nodded. "He put me in his car. A Corvette, and headed south. He said we were going to Mexico, but stopping at an out-of-the-way 'Shangri-La' for the night where he was going to fulfill his fantasies." Debra's voice shook, but she continued. "Lucky for me, he needed to make a phone call at a pay phone outside the motel. Some Mexican drug lord gave him a deadline that could only be kept with fast, straight-through driving."

"A deadline? He was mixed up with the cartel?"

"He'd made a deal with them, and he didn't want to mess it up. Getting away from the motel without being forced to go in with him was a reprieve, but I completely believed I'd die in a horrible crash over a cliff on one of the curves as he exceeded a hundred miles an hour down highway 101. Better than being his slave, I told myself, but I did not want to die."

"Thank God you didn't, Kitten," Paul said, tears in his eyes, as well.

"I had a few minutes of hope when the police tried to stop him in Los Angeles. But it turned into a high-speed chase. Kent managed to evade them by driving through people's yards and fences, over ditches, and finally onto a side road that led him back to the highway to Phoenix and Tucson." Debra looked out the window as she remembered something else. "He fell asleep at the wheel, somewhere in Mexico, wrecking his car and making us even later. With a gun poked in my side, Kent used me as bait to hitch a ride in an old farm truck. A family of five was crowded in the cab, but they let us to sit in the back. It was full of barrels, implements, and animals. I found a space to curl up and fell asleep next to a goat as we bounced along to the next town, where Kent called a guy named Rubio, the drug boss. Rubio was furious that we were late, but he came shortly to pick us up."

"Why did Kent need you in Mexico? What was his deal with the Mexican?" Paul asked.

"Kent, always greedy, I suppose, found an opportunity to expand his drug operation and make even more money. I think it thrilled him to partner with the head honcho of a major cartel. Made him feel important. Rubio wanted to expand distribution in Canada, so he offered Kent a percentage of profits for drugs delivered to key Canadian contacts and an airplane to use for future shipments of the cartel's drugs. Kent could use it for shipping his own product, too. All he lacked was a pilot. And that's where I came in. Turns out he's afraid of flying."

"He always hated airplanes. I'm surprised he even wanted one," Blake said.

"You mean he put you on a plane and expected you to fly back to him when you knew the kind of treatment he had in mind for you?" Paul was incredulous.

"Of course not. He'd demanded that four armed guards fly with me as part of his deal with Rubio. He planned to add them to his workforce once we were back in Canada. He was furious when Rubio only gave him two, but here was no time to argue. Getting out before the feds arrived was the priority. Maybe if we'd gotten there earlier, I would have been allowed to do a preflight check of the airplane."

"You mean two Mexican strong men rode with you to make sure you followed the instructions?" Paul asked.

"An old man and a kid. But as an extra precaution, Kent promised he'd kill both of you and Dad, if I didn't show up at his place on schedule. Since I believed him, that would have been enough to keep me in line."

Debra held up her coffee cup as the waitress came with a full pot, which she left at the table for them.

"You mean you wouldn't have tried to save yourself? But, you knew what he'd do to you," Blake said, as the waitress walked away.

"Yes. But I couldn't have you three killed, and I didn't think Kent was kidding. That's why I was so worried when I couldn't make it."

"What happened?" Paul asked.

"The airplane was an old Beechcraft C-45, a relic from World War I, and looked it, though they insisted it had been thoroughly refurbished. If true, it wasn't obvious. Its underbelly, which they'd painted black, was dented and pockmarked. When I started to do a preflight check, Rubio insisted it had already been done. I don't know if it had, but he was anxious to get me out of there with the payload before the feds showed up. He'd been warned of a raid."

Blake nodded. "Anyone rich enough and criminal enough, including Kent Mallory, has a well-greased early warning system."

"Everything went as planned with a stop in Utah for a delivery. I never made it to the second stop for refueling in Nebraska. Flying over the Rocky Mountains in Colorado, the engines failed, first one and then the other, even though we still had plenty of fuel."

Louis leaned forward. "So that's how you ended up in Jamestown. How did you manage to survive the crash? Good thing it wasn't mid-winter."

"Actually, it was February and very cold with lots of snow."

"But I didn't find you until the end of May."

"Let her tell the story," Blake said.

"We had to jump," Debra began, tears clouding her eyes.

"You okay?" Paul asked, reaching for her arm. "If this is too hard..."

"No. I want to tell it. Maybe confessing will help me sort out the guilt I feel about things that happened next.

Hard, but I need to get it out."

Blake, put his arm around her, drew her closer. Paul reached across the table for her hand, held it gently, and rubbed the back of it with his thumb.

Taking a deep breath, Debra said, "I'll start from where I was feeling good about it all, the plane and my performance as a pilot, enjoying the beauty. A little before noon, the highest peaks of the Rocky Mountains came into view, snow-covered and gleaming in the sun. I held the Beechcraft in a steady climb until reaching the planned cruising altitude. Once there, I throttled back, adjusted the trim, and relaxed. We were cruising at 170 knots, pretty good for the old bomber. I smiled at Don Pedro, the old Mexican assigned to see that I stayed on course. He smiled back and nodded to the seat behind him where Tomás, the kid probably no more than 17, slept, slack-faced, with his gun slipping off his lap. Flying at 12,000 feet, just enough to clear some of the shorter peaks that Rubio, the drug boss, had mapped out for me, had taken its toll on the boy. I knew that without oxygen, we would all be drowsy if we had to fly that high for long, but we soon cleared the divide and dropped to 8,000 feet over the foothills.

"I congratulated myself that everything had gone like clockwork. Flying over mountains is risky in such an old twin engine, yet I felt confident. That's when the left engine coughed once and stopped turning. I automatically feathered the dead engine, shoved the throttle of the right engine, adjusted the trim, and hoped I could make it to a flat place to land with only one engine. But about that time, the right engine sputtered and died. I didn't try to restart it. I adjusted the trim in the hope that the plane would hold a glide. It was time to get out.

"Don Pedro jumped up and ran. He grabbed one of the parachutes and thrust another at Tomás, yelling at him to follow. I reached for a third, but there was none. 'Where is the other parachute?' I screamed, first in English then in Spanish.

"'Solamente dos.' Don Pedro said. Only two. And with a sad smile, he dropped out through the open cargo door."

Debra's eyes clouded again, and in a choked voice said, "Not my proudest moment."

"Go on," Paul said. "You know we won't judge you."

"I glanced at the altimeter. 7,900 feet and dropping fast, and still over rugged terrain. Then, and this is what I'm ashamed of, I lunged at Tomás as he scrambled toward the open door, donning the parachute. I grabbed the chute as he struggled with the straps.

"His fist caught my face, hard, and I fell backward, and he secured the chute. As he hesitated at the open door, I scrambled up and dove, tackling him around the waist and driving us both out of the airplane. I looked down as the ground rushed up to meet us and screamed at Tomás to pull the cord. He seemed petrified. I screamed again three times in Spanish before I finally felt the upward tug as the parachute opened, jerking me so hard that Tomás's pants slipped off his hips. I tightened my grip and slipped down his legs, stopping at the top of his heavy combat boots. If his boots had come off, I'd have fallen to my death. Seconds later, my foot struck a treetop. I scraped through heavy branches of stiff spruce needles, hiding my face between the boy's ankles.

"I heard the resounding crash of the airplane farther

down the mountain, as we stopped abruptly and dangled several feet above ground. The chute got hung up in tree branches. I looked down and guessed I was about twelve feet above the snow-covered ground. I let go.

"Turns out, the mound below me that looked so soft was a slightly buried boulder, hurting my right leg so badly, I thought it must be broken.

"Tomás was screaming. He couldn't get the buckles loose with his weight hanging on the straps, and there was nothing within his reach above or below to brace himself on. He couldn't get loose, and he begged me to help him.

"I wanted to, but I could barely walk, let alone climb a tree." Debra fought to keep from crying.

"There was nothing you could do," Sergeant Stanton assured her. "Don't beat yourself up."

"But it was so cold. I knew that if I left—or even if I didn't, I guess—he'd freeze to death, hanging there, bare from the waist down."

"Sweetheart, you had to save yourself. You would have frozen to death too." Blake says, "And what help would that have been?"

"How did you get out of there with a broken leg?" Paul asked.

A woman approaching their table said, "There you are, Sergeant Stanton. The sheriff needs you." She raised her eyebrows at the group who, in her eyes, must have seemed to be having a leisurely party.

Louis sighed and stood. "Better get to work. So glad to meet you, again, Miss Randall. Someday, I want to hear how you survived in the mountains for four months." He put on his hat and followed the woman out the door.

CHAPTER 28

Blake and Paul pressed Debra to continue as soon as Louis was out the door. The waitress approached the table before Debra could pick up the story where she left off.

"You hungry, Deb?" Paul asked.

"Actually I am. I missed brunch by being unconscious."

"Unconscious? What happened?" Blake asked, alarmed.

"I'll get to that," Debra said, and turned to the waitress. "Are you still serving breakfast items?"

"All day," the waitress said, smiling.

"The meals were prettier than they were filling at the Prism place, and vegan. I didn't mind, but I'm really hungry for ham and eggs and a side of blueberry hotcakes."

The men ordered hamburgers and urged Debra to go on with her story as the waitress left the table.

"Let's see, where was I?"

"You'd just jumped out of an airplane."

"Like I said, it was very cold. My toes were already turning numb. Cowboy boots have no insulation whatsoever. I told Tomás to call Don Pedro, but if the old man could hear, wouldn't he have already answered? Tomás probably thought the same thing. Anyway, I started crawling, dragging my bad leg."

"So how far did you crawl before you found help?" Paul asked.

"Crawling wasn't working. I was just getting my knees

wet and colder, so I pulled myself up on a fallen log and looked around for something to use as a walking stick. I couldn't see more than ten feet in any direction because of all the evergreen trees that covered the mountainside. I began shaking, from the cold—and fear that I was not going to make it. For a minute, I just sat there, clutching my prism, wishing I'd lose consciousness—anything to escape the pain in my leg, my face, and my freezing toes.

"Instead, I heard a twig snap in the distance. I strained to listen and heard just a whisper of footsteps. A wild animal, was my first thought, and sure enough, a huge cat came straight at me. Just when I thought I was cat food, I heard a voice.

"'Well, well, Bobby. What do we have here?' the voice rumbled. Then a big man with lots of gray hair down his back and a heavy, gray beard that hung to his waist stepped out of the trees. 'You okay, missy? Looks like you could use some help,' he said.

"I told him I thought my leg was broken, and he slipped a fur off his shoulders, spread it on the ground, and told me to get on it. 'I'll pull you down the mountain,' he said.

"He asked if anyone else survived the crash. I told him Tomás needed help, and I didn't know where the old man was.

"He said he'd take me back to his place and then come back for the others.

"It didn't take long to slide downhill to a small cabin. The cat bounded along beside me, just like a house cat with a new plaything. The man carried me inside where a fire burned in a stove made from a thirty-gallon barrel. It warmed the small room.

"'Curl up here behind the stove,' he said.' Warmest place in the house.' And he grabbed a pillow and several blankets from the nearby bed, and covered me. The cat lay against me, and the man said, 'Good boy, Bobby. Get the lady warm.' Then he left."

"What kind of cat was it? Were you scared?" Blake asked.

"A big bobcat. I was scared at first, but once I was sure he wasn't going to eat me, I was glad for his presence, as I drew both heat and comfort from his furry body. When I finally quit shivering, I fell asleep and dreamed of cats carrying machine guns.

"When I awoke, the bearded man sat on a chair, looking down at me, sipping something steaming from a metal cup. 'I think you'll make it,' he said. 'Now you're awake, I'll take a look at that bad leg.'

"I winced when he pulled the covers back and tried to get my boot off. I braced myself, but my right boot was so tight, it wouldn't budge. I didn't mean to, but I yelped, it hurt so badly. He tried the left one, and it slipped off easily.

"He went back to the right foot and asked if I wanted a stick to bite on. I shook my head and braced myself. If I fainted it would be a blessing. I should have taken the stick! It hurt like hell when he gripped my knee with one hand and pulled hard on the heel of my boot, then the toe, then the heel again, until it came off with a jerk.

"He whistled, and I rose up on my elbows to look at it. My ankle was huge, mottled blue and purple and yellow. He told me not to move, as if I had any intention of going anywhere. Then he went out and filled a pillowcase full of snow. He put it around my ankle and wrapped it with a towel. I thought the cold would be the worst thing I could feel after nearly freezing to death, but it wasn't. It really did ease the pain.

"I asked if he found the others, and he said he found the one in the tree and brought him in. He was still alive, but in danger of dying from hypothermia. He didn't find Don Pedro, and it was getting too dark to see anymore. He said he'd go back in the morning. I figured that unless Don Pedro started walking out as soon as he landed, he'd be frozen by morning.

"Who was this guy? Where's his cabin?" Paul asked.

"His name is George Pierson, formerly a successful businessman from Denver. His wife divorced him many years ago. He gave her the house and everything they owned except a small savings account and an old Jeep pickup. He bought ten acres of land in the mountains a few miles above Jamestown. He tries to keep it hidden. There are no obvious trails in and out. His cabin is half dugout and the other half log with a sod roof so that it's not obvious from the air. He has a root cellar and an out-house, hidden in the trees."

"Sounds like a disgruntled hermit who might not be so welcoming. Did he treat you okay?" Paul said.

"A recluse for sure. Pretty proud of himself for being self-sufficient, but he must have been lonely, because he didn't want me to leave."

"Is that why you stayed three or four months with him? Had you lost your memory at that time?" Paul asked.

"Hey, my breakfast is getting cold," Debra said. "Let me finish these pancakes, and I'll explain."

"Oh, sorry, we've been keeping you from eating,"

Blake said. "I just want to know about everything you've been through since I deserted you."

Debra looked at him sharply. "You didn't desert me, as much as I ran you off. But, that's behind us. Thankfully."

Debra ate the rest of her meal with another cup of coffee in silence, thinking of what else she should tell them. *All of it,* she decided.

"Okay," she said, pushing her plate aside. "My memory. No, I hadn't lost it at that point. I still knew who I was, and I was desperate to get to a phone, I was so afraid you'd already be dead, since I didn't come back on schedule."

"So the guy held you against your will?" Blake asked.

"Yeah, sort of. He was very kind, so I didn't suspect it. Whenever I begged to go, he said it was impossible. There was a lot of snow, and we had several snow storms, a few real blizzards, while I was there. I believed him when he said we couldn't get out until spring thaw."

"What about the Mexicans? Did Pierson find the old man?" Paul asked.

"He said he found him dead, that his parachute failed to open."

"Did you believe him?"

"Yes. He showed me the parachute, still packed and the rip cord pulled out of it."

"Were you comfortable? I bet you were going stir crazy." Paul said.

Debra described the interior of the little cabin. "It was small but clean and tidy, just one long room with the stove in the center. A narrow bed stood against the back wall in the dugout section of the room. Crude shelves lined the side walls and contained clothing, blankets, towels, and various household items. There was a window on each side of the front part of the cabin. A cabinet with a sink stood under one of them with a five-gallon bucket beneath the drain hole. Bookshelves filled the wall under and on both sides of the other window. The only other furnishings besides the bed were one rocking chair, a small table, and a wooden ladder-back chair.

"Thankfully, he had books," Debra said. "I read a lot. George said he drives to Boulder once a year to pick up canned food and used books. He does all his cooking on the barrel stove. He melted snow and heated it for washing dishes and cleaning. He even filled a wash tub for me to bathe in and politely went outdoors while I cleaned up."

"You never told us. Did Tomás live?"

"Yes, George rescued him and brought him in by the stove where he lay unconscious for a day and a night. Neither George nor I thought he'd survive, but he did. And got up in the middle of the night, stole a coat and some food and left. It was right before a terrible blizzard. He didn't make it out." Debra shuddered and her eyes filled with tears."

"What?" Paul asked.

"It was awful. The winter was really bad with a lot of storms, like I said, and the food supply Tomás left didn't last with two of us. But somehow, George found meat for us. He told me Bobby caught rabbits, and I think that was true, but as time wore on there was less and less to eat, and then suddenly there was plenty. George said he got a deer, though it didn't taste quite like venison. It got us through the winter." Debra's voice trailed off, and she looked away, unable to talk.

"What is it, Deb?"

"It was May Day, and there was still a lot of snow..."

Debra cleared her throat, wiped at her eyes and began again, "It was a beautiful day outside, fresh snow on the ground, the sun shining, the sky so blue it looked like one could reach up and touch it. We got into a snowball fight, and I was really having fun—until I stuffed snow down his shirt and he tackled me. When I fell, he landed on top of me. Instead of getting up, he started kissing me."

"Oh, no!" Blake murmured.

"I screamed for him to get off, and when he did, I ran, jumped across a narrow, swift-running stream, and blindly ran toward an aspen grove. He kept yelling for me to stop. But I didn't, and what I saw..." Debra took a minute to regain composure while the men waited, eyes wide.

"I ran back out crying, fell down by the stream, and threw up. And then I just crouched there, staring at the water—everything went wavy, the roar in my head crescendoed, and I lost consciousness. When I woke up, I was on his bed. I was afraid that he'd taken advantage of me. But he hadn't. It was the first time I had one of my spells since, well since just before Kent kidnapped me. I've had a few since, and my memory got a little worse each time."

"My god, what did you see? Was it...?"

"I couldn't breathe," Debra gasped, remembering. "But I couldn't take my eyes off them either. Two ghastly corpses, naked, hanging, like your dad hangs deer he's dressing out, Paul. Some of the bones were exposed where flesh had been cut away. Long black hair draped over Tomás's frosted face. Don Pedro's eye sockets were empty, yet they seemed to bore a hole into me pushing me away, yet holding my gaze."

Debra clutched her prism, her face ashen, and looked as if she could faint.

"Let's get out of here," Paul said, as a couple at a nearby table stared at them. "Help her to the car, Blake, while I pay the bill."

CHAPTER 29

Debra admitted to feeling weak and nauseated. "I guess my stomach wasn't ready for so much food after not eating for a couple days."

They rented a room in a nearby motel, so she could rest—away from other ears.

"You okay, now?" Paul asked as he sat on the edge of one double bed. Debra lay on the other, and Blake sat on an overstuffed chair next to her. He'd been so sure that she was dead, he could not take his eyes off her. He never again wanted to let her out of his sight.

Debra stretched, nodded, and finished her story.

"I woke in the cabin, not on the pallet, but on George's bed. My head throbbed and my stomach heaved. I said I was going to throw up, and George rushed in with a bucket and shoved it in front of me just in time. When the retching finally subsided, I lay back on the pillow, trembling. I had a pounding headache as I always do, but a horrible fear, too.

"I asked George if he'd taken advantage of me, because he'd never let me lie on his bed before. I had a deerskin pallet on the floor."

"Did he?" Paul asked, "I'll..."

"No. He said he would never do such a thing, and I know it's true. He did confess to falling in love with me, though, and had hoped that the feeling was mutual. He said he would never have kissed me if he hadn't thought it was. He apologized for that.

"But I couldn't wait to get away from him. I couldn't

get the vision of half-eaten corpses out of my mind. My God. I had been eating Tomás and Don Pedro. I never wanted to eat anything again."

"So, your mountain man is a murderer?"

"I asked if he'd killed them."

"Of course, he'd say no," Paul said.

"He said, 'No, no. I never killed anyone. The old man was dead when I found him. I told you the truth. His chute didn't open.' He said it with such earnestness and with tears in his eyes, I can't help but believe him. He told me he'd dragged Don Pedro's body to the trees so it couldn't be seen from the air, that he'd intended to bury it as soon as the ground thawed, but we were running out of food. He believed he had no choice in order to keep me from starving."

"Did you agree?"

"Not at the time. I yelled, 'No. Don't put this on me.' But he couldn't understand why I was upset. He said, 'But, dear.' He always called me 'dear.' He said, 'He didn't need his flesh anymore. Don't you see? I hung it in the tree so wild animals wouldn't get it—and then with blizzard after blizzard, we needed it.'"

Debra paused and wiped her eyes. "I don't know now if I'd choose between...that...and starving to death. I like living."

"Tomás?" Blake asked.

"I asked if he killed Tomás? He swore he didn't. He claimed he found the boy's body in a snowdrift, frozen solid. He started crying, begging me to believe him. And I do. He has a gentle soul, for all his weirdness."

"Well, he saved your life. He can't be all bad," Paul conceded.

"I know. But it took me a long time to forgive him. I got out of his bed and stayed as far from him as I could, refusing to eat anything at all at first and then only some shriveled potatoes and carrots from his root cellar. Finally, on the twenty-fifth of May, George said we could go to town the next day.

"I had come to fear he would never let me go, and had been planning an escape, but I had no idea where to find a town or how far it was. I could have wandered in the mountains until I died.

"He kept his promise, though. He put on snowshoes and had me ride on the deerskin again. It made a pretty good sled as he pulled it downhill. When we got into the trees where the snow was not so deep, I walked. We traveled that way for two hours, with no visible trail, until we came out of the trees at the edge of a bustling little town. George said, 'I see the hippies are flocking in. If you need a ride down to Boulder, I'm sure you can find someone who will take you.' He handed me a ten-dollar bill and said, 'You can make a collect call to your loved ones, and they'll come get you, I'm sure. This should get you something to eat while you're waiting.' He paused and then added, 'You may want to make some calls to the sheriff, too, if you think I deserve it.'

"Did you report him?"

"No. I couldn't see any reason too. Like you said, he saved my life. In his eyes, he'd done nothing wrong, other than keeping me longer than he needed to—but with the weather as it was, maybe he didn't. And even if I'd had the chance to report him, which, as it turned out, I didn't, where would it have gotten me? Two missing Mexicans and an airplane finally identified? George had gone to great lengths to hide all evidence of the crash, camouflaging the plane so it couldn't be detected from the air. And about a week after the crash, a low -flying airplane circled overhead for a couple of days. If I'd reported anything, Rubio and then Kent would know I was alive and where to find me. George saved my life. And other than kissing me that one time—and feeding me human flesh— he was a perfect gentleman."

"But you didn't call us from Jamestown. Did you try?"

"I tried to find a pay phone and was told, everywhere I went, that the phones were out of order. The clerk at the general store told me the whole town was out, 'thanks to the flooding and this awful weather,' she said. I didn't know what she was talking about. It was cloudy, but that's all. She told me a storm was heading their way and was supposed to be socked in by night. Lightning had knocked out phone lines between Jamestown and Boulder."

"Louis said he found you on the side of the road in a late-model, yellow Camaro. How did that happen?"

"For lack of a phone, I did my best to find a ride out of there. I asked just about everyone I met. And there were a lot of people there, mostly out-of-towners. I got lots of weird looks and head shakes for my effort. I finally went into a restaurant and ordered a sandwich. I watched people come and go, and when I finished wolfing down my burger, I approached a group of young people at a large table. When I asked for a ride, one of the girls suggested I take her car to Boulder and she'd ride back with her boyfriend in a couple of days. She told me to leave it at the police station.

"The young man who held her on his lap questioned

her judgment, but she shrugged it off asking, 'What's the worst that can happen? If she runs off with my car, the police will find her and get it back. Or Daddy will buy me a new one. Either way, we both win. She gets her ride to Boulder, and I get to ride with you.'

"She handed me her keys and told me where her new Camaro was parked." Debra shrugged. "She must have had an important daddy!"

Paul said, "Only the mayor of Boulder, according to Stanton. He said he had no idea until she came looking for her car."

"Louis told us you were passed out when he found you," Blake said.

"Yes. It was almost dark when I left town. Low, dark clouds covered the setting sun, and it had started raining. The farther I went the harder it poured. With all that rain, the wipers couldn't keep up. The thunk, thunk of the wipers grew louder, and as you know, rain and running water are triggers for my...you know. The water pouring down the windshield and the rhythmic swishing of the wipers brought on one of the worst feelings yet, hard and fast. I'd barely pulled off the road and stopped before I blacked out.

"I woke up to this horrible tapping on the window. I finally unlocked the door just to stop the noise that was killing my head. It was still raining hard, and the deputy, whom I now know was Louis, was drenched. I was furious that he wouldn't believe I wasn't passed out on drugs and alcohol. I just wanted to drive on down the mountain and find a phone. But he arrested me and put me in his vehicle. I guess he told you the rest of the story."

"Yeah, up until you fell into a stream and almost

drowned, and then woke up in the hospital."

"I remember trying to follow him down the path that was turning into a river. I felt panicked. The crescendo of rushing water was building in my ears. I don't remember falling. I don't know if I hit my head, or if it was just the strength of the feeling that made me lose my memory. But it was complete amnesia. I didn't know where I was, who I was, how I got there, or who Louis was when I woke up in the hospital. And then they let me out. I went to the address I saw on the forms they had me sign. Louis told me I was Tiffany Adams, because that was the name on the registration of the Camaro. I didn't know, but it didn't feel right. I knocked on the front door of a house that was in no way familiar. But I figured if it was mine, the people inside would ask me in and help me remember. Tiffany's mother answered the door, and I immediately knew she didn't know me, so I made up a story about looking for Tiffany. The mother was worried and started asking me questions about her daughter that I couldn't answer so I left, pretending I didn't hear her.

"That must have been terrifying," Blake commented, reaching for her hand.

"Very!" Debra said. "Bad enough to have nothing and nowhere to go, and no money, but to lose oneself is a far deeper loss than I could have imagined. I walked around in near panic. I was always looking for clues, for something familiar."

"Ahh, Kitten," Paul groaned.

Debra touched his arm and gave him a sad but appreciative smile. She continued her story.

"The main streets of Boulder were flooded, and I could tell by the water line it had been much worse. I found a place to sleep in the upstairs of a flooded-out building that wasn't boarded up. The next day I just started walking. Desperately in need of a shower, food, and a better place to stay, I reviewed my options as I walked through the quiet streets. It was chilly so early in the morning, and I was scared. I decided to look for a soup kitchen, or maybe find a business where I could work for food, but I couldn't apply for work looking and smelling like I did. I didn't know when I'd last had a shower, but it had been far too long. Now I know it had been months. The baths in less than two inches of water in the wash tub George provided were rare. But I did appreciate them."

Debra took a sip of water from the glass Blake had placed on the bedside table and pressed on. "As I walked, wondering if it was too early to find any business open, I looked at my watch. It was a little after eight.

"Diamonds on the face of the watch caught the morning sun. When I saw the ring of glistening stones that surrounded the crystal, I figured it was fake. But then I remembered one of the nurses had commented that my watch must be worth thousands. I thought I should be able to sell it for enough to get by until I found a job."

"But, you didn't..." Paul began, anxious to get to the part about the weird place where they'd found her.

"Let her tell it," Blake said, leaning back in the chair. He was enjoying the lilt of her voice, the gleam in her gorgeous green eyes and thought he could listen to her forever.

Debra nodded and smiled at him. "I was walking fast, trying to get warm, and almost collided with a gray-haired man, rushing with his head down. I said, 'Excuse me, sir,' as I dodged him. He looked startled and offended as he came to a quick stop. I asked him if he knew of a place I could get free coffee and something to eat.

"He growled at me to follow him and continued his determined trek down the sidewalk. He led me to an old camper trailer with a few tables and chairs out front. It stood on a vacant lot with a FREE DONUTS AND COFFEE sign over the door. The man ordered me to sit down and went to get us coffee. I slipped into a chair by a vacant table and watched him make his way to the door of the trailer and knock.

"The door opened and a cheery voice yelled, 'Edward, you're late. I thought you might not be coming today.'

"The old man, Edward, pointed at me and ordered two cups of coffee.

"In about the cheeriest voice I've ever heard, the girl promised to bring it right out. She was young; I'd guess 17 or 18, and had a mass of curly red hair and such a smiling, freckled face, I instantly liked her. She carried two cups of steaming coffee and a plate of donuts to the table where the man sat across from me.

"'Going to introduce me to your friend, Edward?' she chirped in a lovely Irish brogue.

"Edward goes, 'No. Don't know her. You'll have to make your own introductions,'" Debra said, imitating his gruff voice.

"The girl's eyebrows shot up, but only for a second. She smiled with her whole face, if you know what I mean, and said, 'I'm Colleen, and I'm happy to have you at our little salvation station. Are you displaced by the flood?'

"I just said, 'Um, yes. I seem to have lost everything.

"Collen looked sincerely concerned and told me how sorry she was, but assured me I was not alone; that the flood has devastated a lot of people. Then she asked my name.

"I started to say 'Tiffany," but by then, I knew that wasn't right. For some crazy reason, I said, 'Call me Trudy.'"

"Colleen accepted that with a big smile. 'Trudy, then,' she said, promising to be right back with more coffee. She actually skipped back to the trailer.

"But Edward, wasn't so accepting. He goes, 'Trudy, huh? Good a name as any, right?'

"I asked what he meant and he said, 'You came up with that one on the fly. What's wrong with your real name? You wanted for something?'

"I said, 'Not that I know of. My name is Trudy. May I call you Edward?' I was trying to be friendly.

"He shrugged and said, 'Might as well. It's my name. My guess is your real name starts with a T, but at the last minute you decided not to share it. What crime are you wanted for?'

"Even though I had no idea if it were true or not, I quickly denied it. I was getting a little irritated.

"He got all huffy and told me not to get, 'all het up.' Then he snarfed down his donut and coffee as if it were a race, got up from the table, and strode away.

"Colleen came out and asked where Edward went, and when I told her I was afraid I'd offended him, she said, 'Don't think a thing about it, Trudy. He acts offended nine-tenths of the time. I don't think he's happy unless he can be mad at somebody.'"

Debra smiled and said, "By then, there weren't any other patrons, so she asked if she could sit and visit, and urged me to have another donut. I thanked her and asked if she could tell me where I might find a pawnshop?

"She started giving me directions, but then she noticed my prism and said she didn't think I could get much for it because there was a place over on 17th that gives them away."

"The PRISM place where we found you," Paul said.

"Yep. She told me she thought it was kind of religious organization, but didn't know much about it. She said it helped her friend find out who she was.

"I guess because of my amnesia, I asked, 'She didn't know who she was?'

"I realized my mistake right away, but Colleen said, 'Well, I don't mean literally. She knew her name and where she came from, of course.' Then she giggled and pointed at me as she covered her mouth with one hand. When she finally got her laughter under control, she said, 'You should have seen the look on your face. You actually thought I meant she didn't know who she was, like she had amnesia, or something. I don't think that happens in real life.'

"I didn't correct her, but when I didn't smile, she apologized for laughing. Then she saw my watch and got all excited. Once she verified it was a Rolex, she said I must be the richest person she knew, and she grilled me about how could I really have lost everything. I must have savings. When I didn't answer she apologized and told me how to get to the pawn shop. She said I'd pass the PRISM place first. I did, and when I saw a replica of my prism in the stained-glass window of the door, I had to find out, so I knocked. You know the rest."

"How long were you there?" Paul asked.

"About a month, I guess. It was a six-weeks session,

and I got there at the beginning of it."

"What was it like?" Blake asked. "We're they as weird as they seemed?"

"Weird?" Debra mused. "Yes. Kind of creepy with all the candles and soft music. But who knows where I'd be if I hadn't found it? It connected me to my mother."

CHAPTER 30

The sky outside the window had turned a thousand shades of red, violet, and orange. Debra stared, thinking of the experiences that led her to PRISM, her mother, and her memory.

"You hungry?" Paul asked, following her gaze out the window. "I can't believe it's already past eight."

"I am a little, but I don't want to go out."

"I'll order a pizza, and we won't need to go anywhere."

"Sounds good," Debra said. She used the bathroom while Paul made the call.

Returning to sit on the bed, her back against the wall, she said, "You asked what it was like to be in that place. I guess you saw the entrance door. It was eerie to see my prism copied in their stained-glass window. Were they playing soft flute music when you came in the foyer?"

"Yeah, in the background. It was a little chaotic, and that woman, Rachelle, was not happy about us being there. If not for Louis's badge, she wouldn't have let us in." Paul said.

"Rachelle was the first person I saw. She wore a flowing scarlet gown as she emerged through a curtain of beads. In a melodic voice, she said, 'Welcome to our spring session of Prismatic Studies of Spiritual Discovery, my dear.' She led me to dark maroon-colored room lit only with candles. She introduced herself and started asking me about what made me decide to join the session. I was trying to explain that I knew nothing about that, when she saw my prism. Then she said. 'Oh, wait.

You are already a disciple. Why didn't you say so?'

"I didn't even know my name, so I didn't answer. She asked if I was returning for another session of their six-week program? I stuttered, trying to decide what to say, and she asked my name. That's when I told her I honestly didn't know. She asked a lot of questions before she realized I wasn't kidding, that I had amnesia—for real. Then she urged me to stay for the session, sure they could help me remember. I had no place else to go and no money, clothes, or anything, so I said yes. They took my watch in payment, but let me keep the prism, of course.

"There is a number on the bottom of the prism, and everyone is different. Because mine only had three digits instead of four like they were now issuing, they assumed one of the digits had worn off. They looked up the number, adding a 1 to the beginning and told me my name was Elisabeth someone from Montana.

"The first session was weird. It was for orientation, I guess, or more like a sales pitch. This guy dressed like a monk seemed to be trying to put us in a trance with our prisms. He asked how much we valued our lives, and weren't we worth the $3600.00 to help us find our true selves. A few of the women and the only man to attend left and only five women stayed.

"After that we had a meal, which was delicious, beautifully presented on a long oval table with a lace tablecloth. I was so hungry I could barely keep from gulping down my food. With restraint, I still finished ahead of everyone else.

"Then this paper-thin blonde across from me said, 'I don't eat bread. Would you care for mine?'

"I thanked her and accepted the slice of toasted rye

spread with some kind of soft cheese. I devoured it and was still hungry."

"When had you last eaten?" Paul asked. "Besides the coffee and donuts."

"It seems like there was a little snack food in the cabin, but I'm not sure. Before that, I had a sandwich in Jamestown. Before that I was nearly starved, because I wasn't about to eat any more meat George tried to feed me."

"You've lost weight haven't you," Paul observed. "And you've always been thin. Are you all right?"

"I'm fine," Debra scoffed. "Do you want me to finish the story?"

"Of course. I just worry about you, is all."

"I know." Deb smiled, and went on, "When the meal was over, we were ushered into a small meeting room. We sat on folding chairs in a circle around a coffee table with candles. They really like candles there. We were all asked to introduce ourselves with our names, what we wanted to be called, our age, where we were from, and how we heard of PRISM. There was a Nancy Ann Brower from North Dakota who was twenty-eight years old and went by Nan and her cousin, Mary from Denver, also 28.

"The next woman, the one who shared her bread, had platinum hair with the front braided and pulled back like a tiara over the rest that fell like a shimmering curtain to her tiny waist. Her skin was so fair it seemed translucent. Her eyes were bright blue. Just like in the first session, her voice was passionate and full of dramatic energy."

Debra pitched her voice higher in imitation. "'I'm Mary Mahr, also age twenty-eight. Can you believe it? It must mean something. Maybe it's a magic number. I'm from California, but not originally. I was born in Minnesota and grew up in Nevada, after my parents divorced. I'm into yoga and dance and blah, blah, blah...' She would have gone on all night, I think, but Rachelle interrupted her to ask what she wanted to be called. Then she went on about how Mary is such a plain, common name and begged us to please call her Celeste.

"There was a lady, age 35, named Candace, nickname, Candy, who became my best friend while I was there.

Then it was my turn. I read the card Rachelle had given me and said, 'I am Elisabeth Martin from Missoula, Montana, and I guess I'm thirty-five, too. And, uh, I believe I'd prefer to be called Beth.' Of course, the name did nothing to jog my memory. And neither did Montana, but Rachelle said it might take some time coming back to me.

"We were each given a daily schedule that included morning meditation and lecture with Murray, the monk-looking guy, then breakfast, group discussion, private sessions with a counselor, a meeting with a guy who did hypnosis, which I didn't trust, and a session of regression therapy to help us remember our past lives. Pretty funny, since I couldn't remember my present one. There was fresh fruit available throughout the day, and dinner was soup and salad. After eating, we gathered for a séance every evening. Celeste was quick to see and talk to her grandmother and learn that she was somehow her own ancestor. What an actress!

"After that, we could go to bed or to the baths. The baths are lovely, with hot mineral water in private tubs and a larger hot tub. The water comes from underground springs. We were free to take reading material to the garden on the roof during our free time. That might have been nice had there been anything to read besides proselytizing material about their organization

"Nothing jogged my memory, but I knew I wasn't Beth. After a month of trying, I asked my counselor to look up the number on my prism without adding the 1 to the front of it. It turned out to be my mother's, Diana Dupris Randall. That sounded right, but I didn't really regain my memory fully until they insisted it was my turn to call someone up in the séance. I'd been resisting that. The room and the ritual both gave me the creeps. Everyone sat in their usual places around the table where candlelight cast flickering shadows across our faces. Portia, the medium, who looked ghostly in her pale makeup and dark lipstick, started by saying, 'This time I am going to call on a former member of our spiritual community. When I first heard her name, I didn't know whether she had passed on, but a little research revealed that she has.'

"Portia's smile, with her pale face and black lips and eyeshadow, sent a chill up my spine. I grasped my prism and held my breath when Portia said, 'I am calling up the spirit of Diana Dupris Randall, who died of an unfortunate accident many years ago in Texas, leaving behind a baby daughter.' She looked at the ceiling and said, 'Diana, what message do you have for the young woman who sits by my side today? Is this your daughter?'

"They had background music playing as they always do. This time it was just a recording of ocean waves and bird calls. The sound of the waves was getting to me. It was all so eerie, my mind whirled and just like all the other times I've had one of my feelings, the sound of rushing water got louder, and I heard a voice calling my name. But this time I saw bubbles rising from a woman's open mouth. The sound grew until it roared in my head and in the murky water, a woman's face, framed in dark curls, fell away from me and disappeared. Then everything went black."

Both men sat like statues, holding their breath as they strained to hear every word.

"I woke on a bed in a room filled with light that was torture to my aching head. I had to throw up. Someone put a basin under my chin, and helped me roll over. After I vomited, I asked where I was. And Rachelle told me I was in the infirmary. I told her I had my memory back.

"She started telling me how scared she was when Portia couldn't revive me. They called Duane, the hypnotist, and he carried me to the infirmary. She said she and other staff members, taking turns, had sat with me round the clock.

"When I asked how long, she said, 'three days,' then got all defensive, explaining they would have called a doctor or taken me to a hospital, except that my blood pressure, heart rate, and breathing all stayed normal. So, they decided I just needed to sleep. Which was right, but I think she was afraid of getting sued."

"And she should be sued," Paul said. "You could've died while she worried about losing a client. Maybe she was afraid of getting inspected."

"No, Paul. I wasn't about to die. And I did need to sleep it off, just as I always have. And when she asked if she should call my father or the police, I said, 'Don't call anyone; just give me my clothes and let me out of here.' But she argued with me. Told me to rest and something about having a staff meeting. I asked why, and she said, 'Well, we've never allowed anyone to leave before the six weeks were up, so we need to discuss extraordinary circumstances.'

"What?" Paul yelped. "See, we should sue them."

Debra shook her head. "No, I might have threatened to, if they'd tried to detain, me, but you found me."

"And thank God we did," Paul said.

"When she left me alone, I tried both doors. They were locked with a key. I went to the roof to see if I could find a way to climb down, but there wasn't, and I was so weak and tired I lay down on the lounge chair and fell asleep. I was dreaming about riding a horse across the Texas plain and hearing you calling my name. Then I woke up, and it really was you."

CHAPTER 31

Paul lay awake, listening to the soft in-sync breathing of the couple in the other bed. He finally rose, turned on the lamp, and lifted the phone. Debra lay curled in Blake's arms as they spooned together, both sleeping soundly. He'd offered to get a room of his own, or get one for each of them if Debra wanted her privacy. She'd refused. "I want both my boyfriend and my forever best friend right here with me, if you don't mind. I'm sleeping in my clothes and there's room for Blake beside me. Is that all right with you guys?"

They'd all agreed, but Paul was lonely and his thoughts turned homeward. He turned off the lamp and put a call through to his wife. Speaking softly, he said, "Maureen, I miss you. When I get back, please give me another chance. I know I haven't been the best husband, but I think I can be."

By the time he'd hung up the phone tears streamed down his face, but a smile brightened his eyes. "Yes," she'd said. And then she'd given him the news she'd been afraid to tell him until he finished his search.

She was pregnant. "I can't believe it," he whispered, "I'm going to be a father."

When Debra awoke, rested, in the morning, Blake was in the shower, and Paul was sitting at the small table by the window. He had coffee in hand and held up a cup, saying, "I have coffee for all of us—and news I can't wait to tell you."

As Debra sipped her coffee, Paul told her about talking to Maureen.

"Oh, Pablito, I'm so happy." She stood and kissed him on the forehead.

He stood and hugged her.

"You're going to be a father. You'll be the best one ever. And just think, I'll be her auntie!"

"Her?" He laughed and released her. "I was thinking of naming him Paul, Junior."

"Whichever it is, I'll love him or her with all my heart. And I'll do my best to get on Maureen's good side."

"I don't think that will be so hard, now that she's gotten over her jealousy. She was genuinely happy to know you were found alive."

"You told her?"

"She asked, but don't worry. I made her promise not to tell anyone. Not that she talks to your dad or my family much."

Blake came out of the bathroom, dressed, and joined them for coffee, as Paul continued. "Now here's the plan. Blake said he'd take me to San Francisco after he drops you off in LA to confront your dad. I'll pay him whatever a commercial flight would cost."

"Um, wait a minute. I've been thinking about this—a lot," Debra said. "As soon as the world knows I'm alive, Kent will be after me again. He's holding my boys prisoners, and I know he's killed some of them. He has to be stopped. I aim to see the men I brought to him set free."

"And how do you intend to do that, Kitten?" Paul asked.

"We can't go to the authorities," Blake said. "He has informants, as you know, Paul, but Debra," he said, "please let me take you to L A, while I go on to settle the score with my brother."

"No way. You can come with me, but you're not going without me. And Paul, Blake's right. We can't go to the law. It's up to us. Up to *me* to stop him," Debra insisted. "After all, I'm the one who carried innocent young men right into his trap."

"Not entirely innocent if they were running from orders to report for duty," Paul said.

"Don't get me started on that subject. I believe in conscience over tyranny. Civil disobedience is justified when our government tells you to go kill people for no reason other than stroking a president's self-serving ego and padding the pockets of the already rich..."

"I know, I know. I agree with you," Paul said, hands in the air in a gesture of surrender.

"They trusted me. That's what it boils down to. They trusted me, and I let them down. Now I'm going to do something about it. Before I let dad or anyone else know I'm alive."

"So we're going to go to Canada? And what? Kill Kent if we don't get killed first?" Paul asked.

"Not you, Paul. You're going home to Maureen. You have a son or a daughter to take care of, but first, take good care of your wife. It wouldn't do for you to get killed; you have dependents."

"But I can't let you go put yourself in danger without going along to protect you."

"You can, and you will. I insist, Paul. We'll put you on the next plane to San Francisco. But you may not tell anyone what we're planning. Not even that I'm alive. Do you promise?"

"I don't like this at all, Debra. Please. Don't do it. And you're right. I don't really want to put my life on the line right now, but I don't want you risking yours, either."

"I'm going to do what I have to do, Paul. Either you're going back to Maureen with the promise you won't tell, or you can go with us. You just can't screw this up by calling the cops."

"I won't call anyone, but damn it, Debra. This is all wrong."

"Paul," Blake said, breaking into the heated conversation, "How many times in your life have you changed Debra's mind, once she made a decision?"

"Not one single damned time," Paul said with gritted teeth.

"That's what I was afraid of, so I probably won't get anywhere begging her to let me go take care of Kent alone."

Debra knew Blake was talking about her as if she weren't there to get her ire up. It was working. "You're damned right, Blake. I'm going, and I'm going alone if I have to, but you sure as hell are not going without me."

"Then I guess I'll have to go, too," Paul said, his face red with anger. "I can't go back to tell everyone I let you go get yourselves killed while I hid at home like a big coward."

"That's not the way to look at this, Paul," Blake said. "Two is better than three in this case. Debra and I know the lay of the land. We can ambush him. How about this? You go home, give us two days, and if you don't hear from us by day after tomorrow morning, call Garrigan to come investigate. That way, we can get the jump on Kent, but Garrigan can get there in time to save us if anything goes wrong." Blake continued, "Make sense?"

"He's right, Paul," Debra added. "We need someone to know where we are and call for backup if it doesn't go as planned."

"Two days is too long," Paul said.

"No, it isn't. We have to get weapons, make a plan, and get there. We won't be in BC until late tonight or tomorrow morning. Call Garrigan day after tomorrow, if you haven't heard from us."

"You could be dead by then."

"Okay. Call him tomorrow night. But not before 10. Give us time to get to him."

Paul reluctantly agreed. They took him to Stapleton airport in Denver and then went to a gun shop to get Debra a weapon and teach her how to use it. They didn't fuel Blake's plane and head for Canada until evening.

"I just hope your boys are still alive, Debra," Blake said as they took to the skies. "There was no sign of anyone working in the field or the greenhouses when I led Garrigan and the RCMP on a raid of Kent's place. The bunk house was empty. No one was in the house, unless he had them in some hidden basement. He told the Mounties there wasn't one, and they believed him."

"He wouldn't kill them all as long as they're useful to him. My guess is he hid them in the hide-away he made for me. His 'Love Nest' he called it."

"What? You knew about that awful place?" Blake asked.

"He described it in detail as he drove like a madman to Mexico. The main reason he didn't come after me sooner was because he was constructing a building in the forest on the other side of the alfalfa field where no one would

223

see it. It had a full basement—a windowless room that he said had a bed, food, a water supply, and—he was delighted to detail the torture he had in mind for me—a closet full of sex toys, including chains, whips, chokers, and leather restraints."

"It's true. I found it, looking for you. It's why I was so sure you were dead."

Debra nodded. "I'm sorry you had to see that, but I'm glad I never did."

"So, what's our plan. March in there and shoot him when he's not looking"

"Do you think you can kill a man?" Debra asked.

"If it's to keep him from killing you, yes." Blake sounded more angry than confident.

"I'm not sure I can. I'd rather restrain him with handcuffs and ropes until law enforcement can get there."

"All the more chance he'd have to kill both of us," Blake said. "Besides we don't have rope or handcuffs"

Debra looked behind her seat. "Look. Duct tape. That will do."

"All right. We'll land on his place on a road alongside the alfalfa field, not far from thick forest. He'll hear us land and come out there, probably on a motorcycle. We'll have time to disappear into the trees and get a jump on him. I'll go one way and you the other."

"Okay, but if you shoot, try to hit a non-fatal area. Arm or leg, okay?"

"Why give him a time to kill us, if we can stop him," Blake asked.

"It's just that I don't want either of us to have that memory. I'd rather see him rot in prison than die without knowing what hit him."

So would I, Blake thought, *but not at the risk of getting killed before I can save Debra.*

"So, what's your plan?" he asked her.

"I'll step out with a gun on him before he can go for his. Once his hands are in the air and he steps away from his weapon, you can go in with the tape. I'll close in at the same time and help you tie him up. You can shoot to disarm him if he raises his gun instead of dropping it."

"Sounds easier than it's going to be," Blake said, knowing that the reality would probably be entirely different. His main concern was that Debra didn't get killed, and he would be relieved if Kent did. "Fine," he said. "Let's do it."

Landing by the light of the moon that barely illuminated the landing strip, they crowded the alfalfa field to avoid hitting any trees they couldn't see. It made the landing a little rough. Blake killed the engine, and they ran to the trees, barely reaching the shadows before a motorcycle came blasting into the field.

"Is it him?" Debra whispered as she ducked behind a tree.

Blake wasn't sure so he waited.

"Back again, little bro? I still don't have your girlfriend, but I'm willing to take you out anyway. You're becoming quite a nuisance," Kent yelled.

It was too dark to see him clearly, but as Kent strode toward them, Blake didn't wait for Debra, but yelled, "Drop it, Kent. Stop right there, and put your hands in the air."

Kent laughed and kept coming. Blake fired.

Bullets immediately strafed the trees, back and forth, Debra dropped to the ground and lay flat on her belly.

Blake ran to the next tree and fired again.

"Missed me," Kent taunted, "Try again."

And Blake did, from an area farther back. He fired three times. More shots came from Kent's gun. Blasting trees in a semicircle, raining splintered wood down on Debra. She heard a guttural moan from behind her. Blake was down.

Furious, she rolled to her feet and ran from cover, shouting. "Stop right there, Kent Mallory. One more step and you're dead."

"Debra? I'll be damned. What a brave little tiger you are."

She raised the pistol, holding it steady with both hands, but, before she could squeeze the trigger, he was running straight at her, carrying the weapon in his left hand as his right arm dangled lifelessly. She fired but he dove beneath the shot tackling her just above her ankles. She went down, flat on her back, her breath knocked out of her. Kent crouched over her.

"Thanks for coming back to me, sweet thing," he crooned, ignoring the arm that dripped blood on her as he rose to his feet. "God, I love a feisty woman. Let me help you up, darling. You know I'm not going to kill you. Not right away. Going to have some fun with you first. I ought to pull off your clothes and rape you right here for old time's sake. See if your boyfriend comes to your rescue this time, but I have a feeling he won't be moving again."

She rolled away, reaching for the gun she'd dropped.

"Oh, no you don't," he said, stepping on her wrist and stooping to pick it up."

But instead of picking it up, he fell on top of her as a

shot at close range blasted her ears.

Blake, she thought. *He's alive!*

She shoved the still body off her and scrambled to her feet. Instead of seeing Blake, she saw Millie, whose face was pasty white. She had a small revolver in her hand.

CHAPTER 32

Millie dropped the gun and knelt beside Kent's still form. "Is he dead?" she asked.

One look at his dead eyes assured Debra that he was, and Millie confirmed it with her fingers on his carotid artery.

"He's is," she said in a voice with no emotion.

Debra dashed toward the trees yelling Blake's name.

"Over here. I can't walk," Blake yelled back. Debra had never been so glad to hear anyone's voice.

"Where are you? I'm coming."

"Almost to the field. I've been dragging my leg. He must have hit a bone."

Debra knelt beside him. The wound was in his lower leg, and the bleeding was only a trickle. She helped him stand and lean on her as they stumbled into the field of new-growth alfalfa.

Several young men approached, running across the field.

"Let us carry him," came a familiar voice.

Debra whirled toward the voice and scanned the man's face in the moonlight.

"Jake? Is it really you?" She reached her free arm out to him. "I was so sure you were dead. I thought Kent would kill you for talking to me." Tears of relief filled her eyes.

Jake squeezed her arm and got on the other side of Blake to support him, and asked, "Did you kill Sam?"

"I think Millie did," Debra said, looking for the little

woman. "She saved my life."

Together they walked Blake to where Millie stood over Kent's prone form.

"He's dead," Millie repeated. "I shot him through his black heart. My aim was good. He was going to kill you. I knew he would kill me, too, soon. He was tired of me."

Millie wobbled a little, and Debra caught her as she fell. Sitting beside her on the ground, supporting her, Debra watched her blink back to consciousness in the moonlight.

"I don't want to go to jail," Millie said, shaking as Debra held her. "But I couldn't let him keep killing people."

"You won't go to jail. I promise you. You saved me. Thank you. Now I have to take care of Blake." Jake eased him to the ground and Debra sat beside him. "Kent, I mean Sam, shot him in the leg."

"I'll help." Millie knelt over Blake's leg, all signs of weakness gone. "One of you boys go on the motorcycle to the house and get the first aid kit." She told them where to find it, and one of the men took off through the field.

"How did you get here so soon, Millie?" Blake asked as she pushed up his pants leg to look at his wound.

"When Sam started off with the motorcycle in the middle of the night, I woke up. I knew it could only mean trouble, so I got my gun and followed him. My sister bought the gun for me the last time I was in California. I told her I was getting afraid of Sam. He never knew I had the gun, or he would have killed me with it. He would have taken it and laughed at me. Then he would shoot me dead with it."

Debra gasped, "Oh, Millie!"

"It's how he is," Millie said. "He would think it was

funny. I know him." She shivered and continued. "Of course, I couldn't keep up, but I ran as much as I could. I kept hearing gun shots. I saw him knock the lady down." She looked at Debra. "I heard him say what he would do to you. When I saw him reach for your gun, I shot. He never saw me."

The eastern horizon was beginning to lighten when the man on the motorcycle came back with a small metal suitcase. "I was trained to be a nurse. That was before I met Sam. He told me I could be the nurse for his company, but he only wanted to use me to wait on him and give him sex whenever he asked for it. But I always kept my medical supplies, though I hardly ever used more than a small bandage now and then." Millie kept talking as she worked. It seemed that the death of her slave master had loosened her tongue.

While one of the boys held a flashlight, Millie cut Blake's jeans to expose the bullet hole. She cleaned the wound well with alcohol and coated it with iodine. "The bullet is in the bone. The doctor can get it out for you at the hospital."

She wrapped his leg tightly in thick gauze.

While Millie worked, Debra spoke with Jake. "I'm so sorry I got you into this. I really didn't know..."

"I know. I knew you didn't when you came here the first time."

"I'm so relieved that Kent didn't kill you for talking to me."

"He threatened to, but I was his best worker, and he had a big crop ready to harvest and needed all the help he could get. Around the first of March, Sam had us clear all the buildings of drugs, hide them in a load of baled hay, and pull up all the new growth of weed in both greenhouses. He was storming around shouting about his brother calling the cops on him, he said 'the son of a bitch thinks I have his girlfriend.' Then he started cussing about you giving him the slip and if you weren't already dead, he was going to make sure you were if he ever found you. I was afraid you were dead."

"Where were you when I came with the RCMP and a cop from California?" Blake asked, looking up from the ground.

"He crammed us all into this little building up there in the trees where nobody ever goes. We didn't even know it was there. He locked us inside until the cops were all gone. Then he made us work twice as many hours until more plants were started and the labs back in working order. We didn't get much sleep."

"He put me in a tiny space under the house where the water pipes are." Millie shivered. "It was cold and dark, but I could feel the spiders and mice crawling over me. I was afraid he'd leave me to die, but he finally let me out after the police left."

"What's that?" someone asked, looking up. The sound of a helicopter blades, beating the air grew louder.

Soon it came into view, and a floodlight moved across the field from Blake's plane to where they all huddled around Blake, not far from Kent's body. The chopper landed nearby.

"Police!" A voice boomed over a loudspeaker. "Stay where you are. Put your hands in the air and keep them there. Put them down, and we'll shoot."

Everyone but Blake stood, hands high over their heads as a bright light in their faces nearly blinded them.

As armed men approached, the officer in front asked, "Is Kent Mallory present. If you are step forward."

"He's here, but he can't step forward," Jake said. "He's dead."

The officer lowered his gun and asked. "Is Debra Randall here?"

"I am, sir. My boyfriend has been shot, and this woman is dressing his wound. We need to get him to a hospital."

"Debra, Kitten, Oh, thank God you're alive," Paul shouted as he ran to her, grabbed her by the waist and swung her in a circle before hugging her close to him. "Oh, I'm sorry. What if you were hurt? Are you hurt?" He held her at arm's length and looked at her in the predawn light.

"I'm not hurt, and I'm glad to see you too, Pablito. And you saved us a telephone call."

"I couldn't wait as long as you asked me to. I didn't think you considered how long it would take for law enforcement in two countries to get organized. I called Garrigan as soon as I landed." Paul rushed through his confession, as if compelled by guilt.

Pat Garrigan stepped forward, "So you are the mysterious Miss Randall. Though we've never met, I feel like I know you. I have a lot of questions, but first, let me say how glad I am to see you alive. I feel like I just witnessed a miracle." It looked like it too, as the rising sun shone through her windblown hair, forming a golden halo.

"I'm glad to meet you, too," Debra said, extending her hand. "I'd stay and chat, but I need to fly my boyfriend to a hospital, if someone can help me get him in the plane."

"We have a body here, and therefore a crime scene,"

said the Mountie, "We'll need to ask questions."

Debra started to argue, but Garrigan intervened. "Better let them get Blake to the hospital. He doesn't look too good. I can vouch for them not being flight risks. You can question those here and talk to these two at the hospital later."

"I'm going with you," Paul said, rushing to help Blake limp to the airplane.

"Mallory," Garrigan yelled. "I owe you an apology. I should have believed you."

As Debra started toward the Cessna, she heard Millie say. "I shot him, but I don't want to go to jail. Please."

Debra turned back. "If it weren't for Millie, I'd be the dead one. She saved my life. And these guys can tell you Kent was a killer."

"Yeah," Jake said. "I can show you the graves where Sam, er, I guess his name is Kent, made us bury the guys he shot when they tried to escape. Whatever happens to the rest of us can't be as bad as the hell he put us through."

CHAPTER 33

Josh Randall breezed into his office to pick up his mail. There should be an answer from Westinghouse, where he'd sent a template for a newly designed motor for the tail section of the stealth plane, a prototype for the Army. If it turned out to be half as good as he expected, he'd beat out all competitors, hands down, and get a government contract that would put him and his family on easy street for the rest of his and Debra's lives. A twinge shot through his chest as he remembered he had no daughter. His precious Debra dead and buried somewhere in the Canadian Rocky Mountains. *Damn Blake Mallory for withholding information, robbing law enforcement of the chance to save her.*

He squelched the feeling that threatened to bring him to tears every time he thought of Debra. He coped by working harder than ever, concentrating on a new airplane design. It's how he'd always compensated for losses in his life. It wasn't working very well.

"Hello, Dad."

Josh stopped, eyes wide. He couldn't have heard Deb's voice. He must be having hallucinations. Ann had warned him that stuffing his feelings instead of dealing with his loss would only make things worse in the long run.

Like a phantom, she rose from a chair in a dark corner and moved toward him.

His knees buckled. His heart pounded. His head swam. "Debra?" he croaked, grasping the edge of his desk.

"Dad," she yelped, rushing to him. "I didn't mean to give you a heart attack. Sit down. Are you okay? Should I call...?"

"No, don't call anyone. Just tell me I'm not seeing things. Is it really you? You're alive? You're here." His voice trembled as she eased him into the chair behind his desk. He clung to her arm, staring into her face.

"I'm sorry, Dad. I couldn't let you know I was coming. I have so many questions that I have to ask you face to face. You have to answer me this time. You have to tell me everything."

He swallowed and nodded.

She studied his face. "Are you okay?"

"Yes. More than okay. You're alive." He stood and pulled her close. "I have to prove to myself I'm not imagining you."

She let her head rest against his chest and savored a hug that she'd longed for but had never received from him until now.

"Let's sit," she finally said, pulling a chair close to his.

He nodded and sank shakily into his plush chair.

"Okay. I'll start with what I know. What I finally remembered. Then you must fill in the blanks," Debra said as tears flowed down her cheeks. She'd planned to be completely firm and to let her anger show. But that emotion had deserted her. In its place was the realization that, in spite his stern demeanor, her father genuinely loved her.

"Dad, my mother drowned, didn't she? And it wasn't an accident."

"Debra," he began, pain written all over his face.

"No, Dad. We have to do this. I remember seeing her. I followed her to the river."

"You can't possibly remember. You weren't even two years old."

"But I do. She was wearing a pretty white dress, the soft, billowy kind. But it had pockets, and she was putting rocks in them. I thought she was collecting pretty rocks, and I wanted to help, so I picked up a rock, too, and handed it to her."

Josh gasped.

Debra nodded and continued, watching her father's face. "When she saw me, she said, 'No, go home.' But I told her I wanted to help. I picked up another rock. She got down on her knees then. She was crying, but she was smiling, too. 'Be a darling, Debra,' she said. 'Take this pretty to Nana.' She took her prism pendent from around her neck and handed it to me." Debra pulled the prism over her head. "This one," she said and held it to the light. "It made rainbows on the grass and rocks. I was fascinated. Then she promised me I could have it for keeps if I would go show it to Nana. I started back toward the house. When I looked back, Mama was gone." Debra's voice caught, but she went on, "I ran back to find her. I got to the river's edge and looked down, and there she was. Her face was under the water looking up. Her eyes were open. Bubbles came from her mouth, and it looked like she was saying, 'Go away,' but she kept sinking deeper, going away from me. I reached for her." Debra looked at her father, falling on her knees beside his chair, "And that is the last that I remember."

She stared into her father's ghostly-white face, gripping his arm so hard her knuckles were white. "I fell in, didn't I?"

He nodded.

"Who saved me?"

"Esther, the woman you called Nana, our housekeeper at the time. She went looking for you and saw you topple over the bank. She ran, but it was some distance. She grabbed your dress and pulled you out, but you weren't breathing. She screamed and a farmhand who knew first aid worked you over and got you breathing again. He took you to the hospital, and the housekeeper called me in LA."

"Why, Dad?" Debra asked. "Why did she kill herself?"

"Don't you think I've asked myself that question a million times? And the bigger question: Was it my fault?"

"Was it?"

"You tell me. I loved her with everything I had. I tried to give her everything she needed." A shudder shook Josh's whole body as he sighed. "But I saw her weaknesses, and I wanted to fix her. I thought I could."

"What weaknesses?"

"Debbie, I..."

"Dad. I can understand why you wouldn't want to tell a child how her mother died, but I'm not a child. I'm her flesh and blood. I carry her genes, so I have a right to know. Everything."

Josh looked beaten as he held his face in his hands, elbows propped on the desk. "You do," he said, finally. "I was so damned angry at her for taking the coward's way out—and almost taking you with her. For leaving us. I could understand her leaving me, if she was that unhappy, but to leave you was unforgivable." Josh's voice cracked, and he looked at Debra with tear-filled eyes, beseeching her to understand.

"Just tell me about her. Please? What were the weaknesses you saw in her?"

"She..." Josh seemed to be searching for words. "She had such unattainable ideals that she was always sad—broken-hearted, really—when she failed to reach them. She'd cry for days sometimes. She always wanted me to do more, and I gave her a lot of money to donate to the causes she joined in her efforts to save the world."

Josh shook his head slowly. "But it was never enough. She started helping all the down-and-outers she found on the streets, bringing them home with her. I thought it would quit when she moved to the ranch. But even though she was pregnant and starting to show, she somehow found them, mostly sick and abandoned animals, and gave them a place to stay in our house. In at least two cases, maybe more, she brought in homeless people, fed them, and gave them a place to sleep.'

"Where'd she find them, so far from town?"

"Mostly at church, I guess. She kept trying to find a church she liked. Strangers were more than willing to take advantage of her soft heart. It wasn't safe, and I put my foot down."

"Wait," Debra interrupted, remembering the dates in the newspaper. "When did you get the ranch? I thought she lived with you in California first."

"Yes. She came out to finish her senior year of college at UCLA—on my insistence. I was madly in love with her. She never liked the city, but I was convinced she liked being near me. When she told me she was pregnant, I begged her to marry me. She said she would only if she didn't have to live in Los Angeles. So, I bought the ranch, and we got married." He looked questioningly at his daughter, assessing how she'd take the news that she was conceived out of wedlock.

Debbie nodded. "I read the wedding and birth announcements in the paper. I wondered if I was wanted."

"Of course, you were," Josh said defensively. "Maybe the timing wasn't the best, but I always wanted children."

"Okay, go on. When did she start bringing people to the ranch?"

"Not long after we moved in and finished the house. Before you were born. When I realized what she was doing, I put a stop to it. At that time, I was coming home every weekend. When I saw strangers moving around my house. I couldn't stand it. I told her no more visitors. No more bringing home mangy pets, either. She took in every stray dog and cat in the county. The place was overrun with sick and starving animals." Looking at Debra with an unreadable expression, he added, "I got rid of them."

Debra gasped. "How did she take that?"

"She was furious. We had the worst fight we'd ever had. It was the first time she showed any backbone, and I was glad to see it, although I told her she was wrong. I was angry that she couldn't see it."

He shook his head again, remembering, and clenched his jaw. "She left me then. She took money I'd given her for art supplies and anything else she might want. But I told her she couldn't spend it on anyone but herself or the baby."

"Did she tell you where she was going?"

"No. She was gone almost two months. Then she

came back, asking me to forgive her. She said she'd gone to some kind of spiritual retreat in Colorado. According to her, she was a different woman, and she thought she could make me happy. I didn't know I was so damned hard to make happy. I was trying to make *her* happy."

"Was she different?"

"For a while it was wonderful. She was more like the girl I'd known in high school. Fun-loving and witty as well as sweet and kind—and as always, the most beautiful creature on earth."

Debra waited.

"By then she was more than eight months along. She seemed happy about the pregnancy—mostly, I think, because I was so happy. I was thrilled that I was going to have a son to share everything with. Maybe Diana was a little jealous. She was worried, too, that I wouldn't love her without her girlish figure. She hated being so 'fat' but in reality, she was too thin. I worried she was starving you."

As his words sank in, Debra looked up sharply. "I was supposed to be a boy?"

"I was sure you would be, for some reason. I was disappointed at first, but that changed quickly when I held you. My god, I had no idea how beautiful a baby could be or how much I could love anyone until I held you. That love grew as you blossomed, learned to talk, walk, and think for yourself. You were so bright and almost always smiling—except when I had to leave you to go back to work."

"Was my mother happy to have me?"

Josh hesitated for just a second. "Of course, she loved you, but she was scared to death she would break you.

She let others bathe and feed you while she watched, adoring you, but afraid to hold you or take you anywhere alone.

"She almost died when you were born. The doctor told her not to get pregnant again. That seemed to make her feel inadequate. She thought she'd failed me because she couldn't give me the son I'd always wanted."

"Didn't you tell her...?"

"Of course I tried to reassure her, but I don't think she ever believed me. Our relationship really deteriorated after that. I had to be away a lot when we were getting the bugs worked out of a new airplane design. I just took for granted that Diana was happy and busy with you. I failed to notice on my brief visits home that she was getting thinner and more withdrawn. I spent most of my time with you, only seeing much of your mother when we went to bed at night." Josh looked at Debra, deciding how much he should say to his grown daughter. Finally, he surged on, "I wanted to make love to her, but she always had an excuse. I was frustrated and angry. I even wondered if she was having an affair, though there was no reason to think so, other than her rejection of me. I went back to LA in a huff most of the time, and my visits home became less frequent.

"When she complained, I tried to get her to move back to LA so I could see her and you every day. I told her I'd hire all the help she needed. She said she couldn't imagine living there again. She needed space."

Josh looked anguished, pleading with his eyes for understanding. Debra held his gaze, encouraging him to go on.

"I had no idea that she was so depressed she'd consider taking her life. Maybe no one did. At least no one ever told me." Josh paused a moment. "Except Mattie. I got a letter from her a few weeks before Diana died, saying I needed to give Di more freedom. 'Let her get out and work on some of the causes she's worried about.'" Josh sighed. "I don't know if that would have made any difference, but I ignored the letter. That part of Diana never changed. She wanted to make everything better, to right the world, and when she couldn't, she was depressed."

"Did she leave a note?"

"Yes. I saved it along with her paintings and sketches. Did you know she was a talented artist?"

"Yes, Mattie told me. She thought you'd destroyed all her art work."

"I didn't, but I put them away where I'd never have to look at them."

"I want to see them."

"Of course. You will. And you can have them. There is just one that I want to keep for a while. When I die, it will be yours, too, of course."

"Where are they?"

Josh didn't answer. He looked at his watch. "Baby, I'm a half hour late for an important planning meeting. Would it be okay if I show you later? I don't want either of us to be rushed when I do."

"When?"

"Meet me here at 4:30. Can you do that?"

Debra nodded. Josh rose from his chair, wiped his eyes, and straightened his tie. He stood and enveloped Debra in a long embrace before leaving the room without another word.

CHAPTER 34

Josh was waiting for her when Debra arrived at 4:25. "This way," he said. She had expected him to take her somewhere in his car, but he led her to the elevator and down to the basement. She thought she'd been in every room on that level, where business records and blueprints were stored. There was a big drawing room where her father often spent long hours working on airplane designs after everyone else had gone home. The lounge, with table and chairs, a refrigerator, cupboards, a hot plate, and a coffee maker, was often inhabited by workers on break. It was empty now.

Josh led her past all of that. He lifted a large poster of one of his planes. Behind it was a door that Debra had never guessed was there. He opened it with two keys, one for each lock, and pushed it open. Debra gasped as she stepped inside. The wall was lined with beautiful paintings. A table held boxes marked with dates. "Sketches and stories and poetry. All hers," he told her.

"My gosh, Dad! Mother did all of these?"

"And a lot more. She was always painting but was never satisfied. She'd come back the next day and paint over what she'd just finished, finally ripping it up and burning it. So, I started taking them and hiding them before she had a chance to criticize and condemn them the next morning. This is a compilation of years of her work from the time she came to California her senior year until she died. I hid them here from the beginning. These two were left in the house when she died. The suicide

243

note was attached to the back of one of them."

Josh indicated a picture of a beautiful, green-eyed toddler with wispy blonde hair, highlighted by the sunlight. She was smiling and clapping her hands. "That's the one I want to keep," he said.

The other was a man on a horse with mountains in the distance behind him, the sky glowing pink with streaks of orange clouds. It was the best picture of her father Debra had ever seen.

Tears filled her eyes as she looked at each picture. There were dogs, cats, mountains, and prairies—a perfect depiction of the area that cradled the ranch with its sagebrush and mesquite. There was a picture of a young Mattie holding a baby boy.

"Are there any pictures of her?"

"No. She would never even try a self-portrait. She thought that would be egotistical. I asked her to paint a picture of the two of us together. She didn't want to, but said she'd try. If she ever did, she destroyed it before I could see it."

"She could have sold these paintings," Debra said. "They are really good."

"She wouldn't consider it. 'Oh, no,' she'd say. 'No one wants this junk.' Try as I might, I couldn't convince her. Her work was never good enough for her."

Debra looked in one of the boxes, saw that it contained a lot of pencil drawings, and closed the lid. "I want to take a lot of time when I'm alone to look through all of these. But not now. May I see the note she left?"

Josh opened a drawer, took out a key, and opened a wall safe. He pulled out a single piece of plain white paper and handed it to Debra.

Josh, my love, I know I can never please you, and I know that I'm not a good mother. Both you and my sweet angel, Debbie, whom I love with all my heart, will have a better life without me.

I go now, bidding you good-bye and praying that happiness will find you at last.

With deep love,

Di.

Debra stared at the note as tears filled her eyes. Finally, she handed it back to her father. "Did you find this note right away? You told the authorities that her death was accidental."

"No, I didn't find it until after her funeral when I was packing up the pictures to bring back to LA with me." Josh looked at her with the same pleading expression she'd seen several times since she'd confronted him. It was a look that begged forgiveness for the confession he was about to make.

"When Esther called me to tell me Diana was gone and you were in the hospital, I told her not to talk to anyone about it until I got there. I flew home immediately. The first thing I did was to search for the body. I was lucky to find it before anyone else did."

Josh let out a sigh that wracked his whole body. "There were rocks in her dress pockets—lots of them. A pack she wore around her waist was also full of rocks. She made sure she wouldn't be able to save herself. I don't think she ever meant for you to see her."

"No, I'm sure she didn't," Debra said. "But you told the police it was an accident."

"Yes, and I convinced Esther and everyone else on the place that's what it was. Even Mattie believes Diana must have fainted and fallen in, unconscious, for she was prone to trances and fainting spells. If any of them didn't believe it was an accident, they kept it to themselves. Esther told the sheriff she thought Diana must have been trying to save her baby, but she couldn't swim. Actually, Diana was a good swimmer. But if anyone knew that, they didn't question her statement."

"I guess the police believed her."

"They dropped it, whether they believed it or not."

Debra stared at him, but said nothing, deciding that if a bribe was involved, she didn't want to know about it.

Josh at last spoke. "What good would it have done for the world to know she killed herself?"

"None. I understand why you wouldn't want it known."

"Thank you."

"I just wish there were some pictures of her. Don't you even have any wedding pictures?"

"There were some. I don't know what Diana did with them. Probably burned them when she was angry at me."

"Am I like her?"

"You have her beauty, her kind-heartedness, the desire to make the world a better place, but not her weakness. You were always more like me in perseverance. You had spunk and stubbornness. You have never been one to give up when you wanted something."

"Why couldn't you tell me any of this before?"

"I thought that the less you knew about her, the less you'd be like her."

"You loved her, but didn't want me to be like her?"

"I know. It doesn't make sense, but every time I looked at you, I saw her—and it hurt. I determined that you'd be strong and happy, not so damned fragile that I couldn't trust you not to break. When you disappeared, I thought you had. And that I was somehow to blame."

Debra sighed. "Thank you, Dad. For sharing all of this and Mother's story." After a pause, she added. "I'd like for all of us to get together at the ranch soon. You and Ann and Paul, with Mattie and Harry, of course. I feel like I need to spend some time at home with these," She swept the room with a wave of her arm, "before I decide what I'm going to do next."

"I'll have these boxed and sent to the ranch. Let's get everyone together in about two weeks. Will that suit you?"

CHAPTER 35

Debra went to the ranch immediately, overjoyed to be going home in her own airplane again. She spent the next two weeks in the south Texas sun, riding her horse, walking her dog, and sitting on the veranda, looking through the sketches and papers her father had saved. Tears filled her eyes as she gradually became acquainted with her mother through her intricate art and poignant poetry.

Everyone at the party was eager to hear Debra's story. Even Ellen came as Blake's guest, having convinced the federal and Canadian government that she hadn't known of Kent's clandestine operation. She showed them the same letters she'd shown Blake. She was free on bond, awaiting trial for aiding and abetting draft dodgers, but hoping for a light sentence. Neither Debra nor Blake had yet received a warrant for arrest for their participation in getting the men out of the US. They assumed they'd have their day in court. Josh wasn't too worried.

On Blake and Paul's request, and with Josh's agreement, Debra invited Patrick Garrigan to the party. He accepted. Having retired from the force, he said he'd delay his planned fishing trip to Oregon for the sake of hearing Debra's story.

She had been afraid he'd feel like an outsider in the close family gathering, but if he did, it wasn't obvious. She noticed, that Ellen, the other "outsider" went out of her way to include him—or was it vice-versa. Either way, they seemed to be having a good time and getting well acquainted.

Ellen begged Debra to forgive her for getting her involved with a son who had finally convinced her to trust him. "I should have known better, but I didn't," she said.

Paul brought Maureen, hand on her elbow most of the time, with a proud, protective air. Maureen glowed, and seemed truly happy as she gazed at her husband. She told Debra she hoped they could be friends.

"Of course, we will," Debra said. "As long as you don't try to keep me away from my little niece or nephew. I'm truly happy for you and Paul, Maureen."

When everyone finally left to go home or drifted to the various bedrooms, Debra asked Blake if he'd like to sit with her on the veranda in the starlight.

"Sure! Help me hobble out there," he said, picking up his crutches.

"I think there are some misunderstandings we should clear up," Debra began, once they were comfortably seated on the porch swing. "About that Christmas, the worst one of my life, which seems like a decade ago, still..."

"I know. I shouldn't have left you the way I did. I'm sorry I did."

"No, no. It's okay," she said. "I'm the one to apologize. I'm sorry I didn't tell you the whole truth about my so-called migraines. As you know now, they were much more than that. Probably something different altogether. I was horrified when I realized I did things without any memory of what I had done." Debra blushed and lowered her head. "And I was mortified that you had to see that for yourself, the night after Christmas. My 'feelings' are always worse if I drink. I knew I shouldn't. Anyway, I couldn't blame you for leaving."

"I just didn't know what to think," Blake said.

Debra took a deep breath and went on. "A therapist in the place I went to in Boulder told me I seemed to be having something akin to shell shock like veterans of war sometimes suffer. She wondered if some terrible trauma had taken my memory. Now I believe it was the shock of seeing my mother die—and of almost drowning. That also explains why water often brought on my feelings. The closer I got to the memory, the worse they got until I lost my memory altogether." She paused and reached for his hand. "It must have been awful for you that night."

"It was weird, and it scared me, but if it ever happens again, I'll understand."

"I haven't had one since I got my memory back. I don't think I will. But, do you think you could accept me if I'm wrong? I mean if I should get another one and...?"

"Are you proposing to me?" His eyes twinkled as he gazed at her, thinking she looked like a fairy princess in the moonlight.

"No. I'm not." Embarrassed, she playfully slapped his arm, and looked away. "I just thought... I mean..." she stammered.

"Because, if you are," he said, lifting her chin to look deep into her eyes, "the answer is yes."

EPILOGUE

Debra rose with the sun the next morning, while the house slept.

She picked up the prism from the bedside table, put a jacket over her pajamas, and left through the back door. Walking across the wide lawn to the river, she knelt at the water's edge.

Yes, this was the place where she'd seen her mother die so long ago. She peered into the water as she clutched the prism. She heard no voices and saw only her own reflection. She closed her eyes and clearly remembered her mother's bright eyes and her big, sad smile as she'd handed Debra, the toddler, the prism, telling her to take it to Nana.

"I'm returning your prism, Mother. Thank you for it. It helped me find you. I miss you—more than ever, now that I know you. I thought I wouldn't forgive you if I found out you left me on purpose. But I do. I've read your poems and looked at your paintings, and I see your goodness, your desires—and your agony. I think my attachment to this prism was my subconscious, holding on to you. But now I have you in my heart and clearly in my mind, so I don't need it anymore.

"Here, Mother. Your prism."

She dropped the prism pendant on its fine, gold chain into the water and watched it swirl with the eddy and sink out of sight.

ABOUT THE AUTHORS

JOAN MARILYN BOCHMANN
11/21/1934 - 09/26/2013

Joan passed away, the victim of cancer just a couple months shy of her 79th birthday. Her award-winning novel, *Absaroka, Where The Anguish Of A Soldier Meets The Land Of The Crow* was published in the fall of 2005 and is still available at *www.ravenpublishing.net*. She began writing *Prism* years ago, wrote several chapters, started over with a different approach and wrote several more, developing the story's main characters, settings, and background. Then, for reasons never fully explained, she put it aside. When her sister, Janet Muirhead Hill, came to be with her after Joan was diagnosed with cancer, they discussed it, revived it, and Joan attempted to continue the story. When it became apparent that she would not be able to, she asked Janet to finish writing it.

For Janet, it has been a work of love, devotion, and grave responsibility. Her greatest hope is that she has done Joan's writing justice, following Joan's characters through the clues and foreshadowing that Joan introduced, to discover what would happen and solve the mystery.

Seven years and dozens of drafts later, here it is at last.

Janet Muirhead Hill is the author of several children's and young adult novels, which can be viewed at *www.janetmuirheadhill.com*.

Janet has looked up to Joan as her hero, role model, mentor, big sister, and best friend her whole life. Joan's influence and inspiration will live on in Janet's heart forever.

ACKNOWLEDGMENTS

My deepest gratitude goes to my sister, Joan, not only for her faith in my ability to finish the story she began so that her words would not be lost to the world, but also for instilling in me from a very young age the love of books and storytelling; for mentoring and loving me throughout her life, which was cut way too short.

Thanks to her son, Gary Zimmerman, and her daughter, Debra Tanner, for their loving support, encouragement, and understanding of how much this work means to me. Thanks to my grandson, Justen Schaak, the first to read many variations of the manuscript and give honest and helpful criticism, and to the many other supporters and editors who read and commented on various versions, helping me get it right. They include Lee Robison, author and poet; author Craig Lancaster; and my friend, Hal Munger, who is always willing to read and line-edit my work.

Among the many other helpful supporters, too numerous to mention are those who read, pointed out typos, and wrote reviews for this book. Their names are on the cover and in the front pages.

Thanks to my husband, Stan Hill, for giving me space, reassurance, and freedom to write, always.

Thanks to my fellow writers at the Madison County Writers Club for boosting my confidence and helping me improve my craft.

Thanks to one of my favorite artists, Herb Leonhard, for the perfect illustration for the cover.

Though many have helped edit, any remaining errors in the text are the fault of my penchant for continued tweaking.

Janet Muirhead Hill